LANDFALL 247

Dedicated to the memory of Vincent O'Sullivan,
1937—2024

May 2024

Editor Lynley Edmeades

Reviews Editor David Eggleton
Founding Editor Charles Brasch (1909–1973)

Cover: Kate van der Drift, *Apples (after Gabrielle)*, 2023, archival pigment print, 750 x 1000mm.

Published with the assistance of Creative New Zealand.

OTAGO UNIVERSITY PRESS

CONTENTS

- 4   Landfall Young Writers' Essay Competition 2024 Judge's Report, *Lynley Edmeades*
- 6   Fourteen Robyns, *Emma Hughes*
- 10   The Drunken Hedge, *Nick Ascroft*
- 12   In-flight (lovers) of Bristol Street, St Albans, *Ariana Tikao*
- 13   The Case of the Walnut, *Thom Conroy*
- 21   View Near the Western Drain, *Michael Hall*
- 22   Little Colonial, *Maddie Ballard*
- 29   Red River Valley, *Fiona Kidman*
- 30   Birth, *Rose Whitau*
- 31   Paorae, *Chris Holdaway*
- 33   The Great Alpine Highwire Act, *Phoebe Wright*
- 39   Shell Fighting in the Pacific, *Federico Monsalve*
- 40   Baking, *Michelle Elvy*
- 41   Seeing Things, *Lucinda Birch*
- 45   Right Now: A Triolet, *Harry Ricketts*
- 46   art versus the world, *Chris Tse*
- 48   Resort, *Mark Edgecombe*
- 49   with friends like these, *Zephyr Zhang 张挚*
- 50   The End Was Wide Open, *James Pasley*
- 58   Yoke, *Nicholas Wright*
- 59   painting, *Vaughan Rapatahana*
- 61   Self-driving Cars, *Nicola Andrews*
- 62   Mistranslation, *Emma Neale*
- 63   The Children, *Greg Judkins*
- 64   ART PORTFOLIO   *Kate van der Drift*
- 73   A Bit of a Mess, *James O'Sullivan*
- 77   Papering, *Nicola Thorstensen*
- 79   First Charge, *Chris Cantillon*
- 80   Sweetie, *Michelle Duff*
- 85   The Plastisphere, *David Eggleton*
- 86   Underneath it All, *Kristin Kelly*
- 92   Stars on Every Lemon Tree, *Medb Charleton*
- 93   My Mother's Skin, *Wes Lee*
- 94   Playing with Dolls, *Kit Willett*

95   trees, *Brett Cross*
96   ART PORTFOLIO *Ayesha Green*
105 Make Horse Beach, Moloka'i, *Kirby Wright*
106 Denial, *Lorraine Carmody*
112 Petroglyph, *Craig Foltz*
114 The Tōtara at 14 Stanley, *Connie Buchanan*
119 I was born crooked, *Zoë Meager*
120 all our warmth and colour, *Rebecca Ball*
121 The best bird for your return, *Claire Orchard*
122 The Lovely Boys, *Scott Menzies*
126 Mudlarking, *Mikaela Nyman*
128 below the graft, *Nathaniel Calhoun*
129 Geraniums, *Cindy Botha*
130 A singer returns, *Harvey Molloy*

MAKING SPACE: IN COLLABORATION WITH RMIT UNIVERSITY'S non/fictionLab
132 THE EARTH WILL BE FINE, *Mia-Francesca Jones & Lauren Vargo* /
143 RE-POEMING AS A PRACTICE OF MAKING SPACE FOR ALTERNATIVE DOCUMENTARY APPROACHES, *Airini Beautrais & Jessica L. Wilkinson* / 157 AFFIDAMENTO: THE MAKING OF A SHARED WRITTEN ROOM, *Amy Brown & Joan Fleming*

THE LANDFALL REVIEW
170 Landfall Review Online: Books recently reviewed / 171 IAN WEDDE on *Gordon Walters* by Francis Pound / 176 DAVID HERKT on *The Book Collector: Reading and living with literature* by Tony Eyre / 180 SIMONE OETTLI on *Tangi: The 50th anniversary edition* by Witi Ihimaera / 183 BRONWYN WYLIE-GIBB on *Bird Life* by Anna Smaill / 187 HELENE WONG on *Backwaters* by Emma Ling Sidnam / 190 IAIN SHARP on *Rapture: An anthology of performance poetry from Aotearoa New Zealand* edited by Carrie Rudzinski and Grace Iwashita-Taylor, and *Remember Me: Poems to learn by heart from Aotearoa New Zealand* edited by Anne Kennedy

202 CONTRIBUTORS
208 LANDFALL BACKPAGE *Pat Kraus*

LYNLEY EDMEADES

Landfall Young Writers' Essay Competition 2024 Judge's Report

The winning writers of this year's essay competition are wise to our shortcomings: as we devise strategies to counter the various global issues on our doorstep, a younger generation continues to show us the consequences of our not-quite-getting-around-to-it. Why the gratuitous bureaucracy and petty politics when people in Gaza are dying in droves? Who cares if landlords don't get a tax break if there are still people without a home? Why does it matter who owns the rainforest if it's on fire? The questions and concerns of this year's essays go a long way in showing up the immense and increasing absurdity of some of our so-called 'mature' behaviour. As we age, we become more and more inured to the banality of evil, to use Hannah Arendt's words; the messages of these young writers are a gift to help us see this.

 The winner of this year's competition, 'Fourteen Robyns' by **Emma Hughes,** puts a spotlight on austerity and bureaucracy. It recounts the story of a young woman's visit to Family Planning but withholds the reason why she is there in the first place. Of course, one doesn't have to reach too far to imagine why she might be there, but the attention of the protagonist towards her surroundings provides a kind of portrait of the setting and its inhabitants, subtly asking: *why does it have to be like this?* It shows immense skill as a writer to say so little about oneself, to extol any opinions or explicitly state 'what' the essay is about, particularly in the 'personal essay' space (that so often lends itself to confessional or didactic tones). In the awkward liminality of the waiting room, we take in all that Hughes notices: the effusive receptionist, a heavily pregnant patient, a tired mother with a toddler, a mother with her teenage daughter, a woman with a black eye and a limp. There is something of the anthropologist's eye here, a gaze that allows the writer the knowledge that there is a reality bigger than her own. Hughes' observations urge the reader to absorb something of the atmosphere of the place: 'cushions covered in felt tip marks and the windows without curtains'; an old magazine with a 'tattered Reese Witherspoon' on the cover, her hair given 'red dip dye'; the plea printed in bright purple capital letters at the bottom of the form she's filling out with her personal details: 'Family Planning needs your help.' More tellingly perhaps, the writer spots 'a little family drawn with red crayon on the striped wallpaper. A mum and a dad and two girls.' A few lines later, the mood shifts: 'I look at the crayon family on the wall, staring hard until my eyes blur with tears, watching the family disappear one by one.' There are layers of quiet comment here: failing public services; the intergenerational transmission of heteronormativity; the inability of some individuals to uphold the status quo or process their own inter-generational trauma (why are the family members 'disappearing'?).

But the real clincher for me is the subtle comment on the tension that lies between third- and fourth-wave feminist movements. In the first paragraph, Robyn, the upbeat and demonstrative receptionist, tells Hughes that 'the nurse will see you soon, lucky girl!' Robyn repeats the phrase when the nurse is ready to see her—'Alright love? You're up … See!! Lucky girl!!' Robyn is old guard, representing an earlier feminism in which young women are 'lucky' to have a service like this. The essay's protagonist, in a state of desperation and confusion, wonders what is so lucky about having to come to a place like this, with its disenfranchised clientele and post-austerity beige. The latter has all the trappings of what those earlier feminists fought so hard for—sexual liberation, free contraception, anonymity of sex education and services—and yet. And yet. We could attribute the tight grip of pathological optimism solely to this idiosyncratic receptionist. But we all know, or have known, a Robyn. Indeed, there are fourteen of them around the country, as the title of the essay tells us. Hughes' essay is spare, touching, and shows a writer with immense potential.

Second place: 'Revenge Fantasy' by **Sherry Zhang**

Highly commended: 'Frankenstein Diaries: A lyric essay' by **Cadence Chung**; 'Good Music' by **Grace Bridle**

Commended: 'An Olive in Gaza' by **Huda El-Shareif**; 'The Things We Inherit' by **Tessa Smith**; 'Social Media and the Fullness of Infinity' by **Ashton McGarvie**; 'Noah's Ark' by **Isabelle Lloydd**

EMMA HUGHES

Fourteen Robyns

There are fourteen Robyns nationwide across all the clinics!, jokes the receptionist, whose name is Robyn. Her name tag is upside down on her lilac blouse. *It's a prerequisite on the job application.* I smile down at the forms she hands me, fingering the te reo Māori. Family planning. Robyn asks if I would like some water; I realise I'm still standing with her at reception. It's hot today, and I'm late and sweaty as I couldn't find the clinic. *We're usually tucked away, dear*, she says when I apologise again for being late. *It's easier that way*, she says, gesturing over to the waiting room. All women. *Take a seat*, says Robyn, tapping at her keyboard, *the nurse will see you soon, lucky girl!* Lucky girl. My chest is tight as I head to the waiting room.

    The nurse wheels out from observation room 2, calls my name and says she'll be there soon. Okay, I smile back at her as she uses the wall to push her chair back into the room. There are gold stars stitched into her sneakers. Her laces are pink, but they look dirty in the sun. I wonder if this is another Robyn or if perhaps they've evenly dispersed the Robyns across the country so as not to overpopulate the Robyns in one area. Maybe there's a clinic operated solely by Robyns. Robyn-powered women centres, sorting the invoices, ringing ACC, washing the blood out with cold water.

    Robyn brings me a glass of water, moving the crumpled magazines to set it beside me. It slops over the side a bit, a few drops on my jeans and on the carpet. *What am I like, ladies? What am I like?* She throws her arms up in the air. Orchestral, she swirls around the room. I laugh, it's genuine. I relax into my seat and uncross my legs. Robyn jollies back to reception to get some paper towels to mop me up, pinching the cheek of a toddler who is crawling at my feet as she gets up. The kid, who couldn't be older than two, keeps rubbing her eyes. I notice her Mum doing the same when I look up at her. *Sorry sorry* she says warily, grabbing an abacus to distract the kid. *Look!!!*, she says, shimmying the toy in front of the girl's face. The colors have been slobbered beige and there is a row missing. The kid looks disinterested but leaves me and wraps herself around her mum's leg, sliding the knobs backwards with one hand, using the other to rub at her eyes. *Sorry*, she says again, nodding quickly at me. I say nothing and nod back.

My eyes can't quite piece together what I'm seeing. Everything in this room looks worn, with various yellowing shades of lime green, purple and orange. It looks like a thousand different rooms pieced together. The most modern-looking thing here is the HIV pamphlets. I like to laugh at the tag lines. What are YOU doing to protect YOU? Let's STOP bullying in classrooms, LOVE EACH OTHER and use CONDOMS. What do you do when your son has a BISCUIT PROBLEM? The flashy pamphlets look alien in the worn environment. (When your child has a biscuit problem, suggest giving them a bowl of plain Greek yoghurt and chopping the biscuit up in it.)

The clinic looks like your everyday suburban GP's office, without the fish, the old people and crutches discarded everywhere. The place also doesn't have the bustle and stress of your standard medical practice. The children here, like abacus girl, look subdued and exhausted with the mums to match. I'm young, but not the youngest here. There is a teenage girl with her mum. The mum is glued to her phone and dressed in all black. She's all business and clearly in the middle of the working day. The teenage girl has a trendy tracksuit on, forest green. Hoop earrings, eyeliner and Birkenstocks. She has wide brown eyes that keep darting around the room. Her toes, painted red, are bony, but her face is round. No phone, she stares into the room. She looks scared. We've caught eyes a few times. I wonder if she thinks I'm scared. At what age do you start to realise the truth of situations? The woman next to her has a black eye.

I distract myself with the paperwork. I don't like the way my name looks in capitals. My name doesn't look like my name in those small boxes. I move down the form. No health conditions, no medication, put Mum down as my emergency contact number—always. I recall drunken conversations with my girlfriends in BYO toilets, freshening up our lip gloss, loudly discussing Dutch men and our OEs. Will you be my emergency contact number in Venice? I'll be your emergency contact in any and every fuckin' country, my girl. Still, for now, I put Mum down—we're far from Venice.

Family planning needs your help, is printed at the bottom of the form, with the option to donate. $20, $40, $60. Or write your own sum. This is the only lettering on the page that is not black, but bright purple and in capitals. Family planning needs your help. I wonder how much money comes from these donations. I look at the cushions covered in felt tip marks and the windows without curtains and find my answer. I see no felts, but everything here is drawn on. Wrapped around, touched. A tattered Reese Witherspoon has been given red dip dye, the carpets have been spilled over with cocktails of playdough and pens. There are a few lamps dotted round, some on some off—emanating various levels of sandy light. It's a very homely headache. I spot a little family drawn with red crayon on the striped wallpaper. A mum and a dad and two girls. The mum has mad curls, the dad no hair at all. I shift in my seat and my chest gets tighter. Black-eye woman has been called in; she is also limping. Her jeans have rhinestone butterflies on the bum, with half the wings fallen off. The mother and the teenage daughter exchange a look in her absence. Expressionless, the girl picks up one of the butterfly gems left on the woman's seat, turning it over and over in her hands.

 I've completed the forms and head back up to reception. No Robyn, but another patient. She has a floor-length floral dress, flaming red hair and is heavily pregnant. Clearly worried, her eyebrows frown down into the middle of her face. She fiddles at the desk, clasping an un-rung bell. I return to my seat, feeling woozy. After this newest patient has been paperworked by Robyn she sits down with the rest of us and puts her head straight in her hands, clipboard falling to the floor. Why is she here alone? Robyn seems unfazed as she steers towards us, a seasoned pilot in tropical turbulence. She brings water, kneeling and murmuring softly. The woman lets out a little laugh and puts her phone in her bag. More settled, I notice she's stroking her stomach in figure eights. I look at the crayon family on the wall, staring hard until my eyes blur with tears, watching the family disappear one by one.

 I guess this is business as usual. Ladies coming in limping, pregnant and underage. If you've waited three weeks, you'll wait another 35 minutes. When you phone to book, Line 1 is contraception. Line 2 is abortions. Recorded voices don't waiver when they tell you that if you are in immediate danger, you need to call 111. I wince at the calls I've made to family planning over the years. The long-winded, often tearful rambles. It's as hard to get here as it is to be here. So, we park early. We arrive late and desperate—saying sorry before we say hello. And once more again before we say thank you.

Black-eye woman resurfaces. Her demeanour is softer. She goes to reception to settle. *On the house today love!* Robyn chirps. *You take care of yourself now. You ring if there's any trouble at all.* Robyn makes her way round her desk and hugs the woman, the woman hugs back, hard. My chest eases. I hear the windchimes at the door as she leaves, rhinestones in her wake, Robyn at her heels.

Alright, love? You're up! The nurse rolls out of her room to call me. I stand up, quickly stuffing my headphones and jumper into my bag. As I turn to head into the room, I catch Robyn's eye and smile back. *See?* Robyn calls. *Lucky girl!*

Lucky girl.

NICK ASCROFT

The Drunken Hedge

The drunken hedge stumbles
into you as you make your driveway
and you lie there and sleep, five minutes,

seven minutes.
After whatever unconscious period of minutes—
though you drag yourself back up to half mast

and swing indoors—
part of you will always remain asleep
at the base of the hedge, forever raising yourself

up out of it, thinking, well, I was asleep there.
Tunnelling inside and into bed, your
carefulness drunk too but still careful,

the ceiling turns
with the sound of sleep breathing, heavy and long
with the out-breaths, whispers and whistles

on the in.
All of your mouth sounds are loud.
The inner cheek sucks and squelches.

There is a piece of olive wedged behind a canine
your tongue works at like an octopus.
The heartbeat in your ears is tympanic,

signalling tone shift.
At work the next week you are still asleep in a bush
and, realising, stagger inside, mud on your forehead,

a leaf in your fringe.
The pillow bristles and you disappear,
reappearing horizontal on the driveway verge,

thinking, here I am then.

ARIANA TIKAO

In-flight (lovers) of Bristol Street, St Albans

(after a painting by Ruby Wilkinson, 2023, Jhana Miller Gallery)

i.
the young sparrows shacked up in the shit-dripped
spouting of our neighbour's tile roof

were mating so wildly all feathers and flap
& fell onto our deck with a thud

their small beige bodies still attached
to one another, but somehow

managed to survive and now they've young
beaks to feed and cautionary tales to tell

ii.
a pūrerehua spins   catching air   like wings
fricative   feathers   sing   a   flickering
curvy slivers of   light inside   a   camera's
shutter   controlling   contrast   and what
we   see   and   what we   don't

   do   you   have   a   fear   of   flight?

in dreams   I run   both arms   reach out from
their   sides   I   flap   and jump   and feel
my body rise   as   if   a gust of hot wind
is lifting it up   like the Ascension
except   if I could (in a dream)   I'd be sweating
     but Jesus   always looks   so hellova serene

THOM CONROY

The Case of the Walnut

It was something that had happened, or it was something that would happen in the future. Once he'd felt absolutely certain that he'd encountered it directly. Felt it descend or something similar had occurred, like maybe he'd almost dashed past it without stopping to have a look so that it seemed to be merely the darkest part of shade from an enormous tree. Other times he felt he could stalk it in the way you might sneak up on a wolf that you find napping under a window at the end of the hallway.

Unaccountably, when it lay bare and of itself, it appeared as one half of a walnut's carapace.

★

There was a woman, you know that story. He always said that and so did she. What did the two of them need with anything whatsoever that could not be happening at this moment, now and here? All they needed was within reach, was it not? A tiny little world no larger than a bed.

Looking in on the two of them was like lifting a lid to a little pot. Inside the little pot were the bed and the floor strewn with books and records like the floors of so many rooms once strewn with books and records. You might see them laughing. This would be likely. Or baring their claws. His voice could be heard from two storeys down, she said.

Pull yourself together, she said.

They were followers who believed themselves leaders. Sometimes they pictured themselves at podiums in the future or waving from the back of cars in the service of something they knew was slipping away. Every hour that passed, it was further from your grasp.

And when you next lifted the pot, it was just him. Not on the bed but sitting like a shirtless scarecrow at a fibre-board desk, woozy, pimple-cheeked, a book open in his hands even though the room had fallen—whoosh like that—into darkness.

★

A man called Liam came into his life, and for a short time they sought together. At least they might have been seeking together. Looking back, he was never sure. What he knew was that Liam would bring a hunting rifle or he would use a hammer or a tin of shiny axle grease. He had a rollicking mad sense of humour, and this fact seemed quite important for much too long.

Once when he told Liam about wanting to speak at podiums, Liam had turned to him and said, What would you be speaking about?

He couldn't say. Or he partly could, but it was hard to articulate. Didn't Liam think so? How would Liam describe it?

As *out there*, Liam said, speaking of it from behind his place at the wheel of the Jeep he'd borrowed from his father. Liam was like that, having a father to borrow from—and not only Jeeps and axle grease but honest to God dreams and ambitions so presupposing they might have been the dreams of an entire people. How safe, how lofty it felt to sit in the passenger seat of a Jeep with a man like that and be told it was *out there*, as if it were a boulder in a boulder field or a cloud or an ever-descending giant squid.

Yes, he thought, this was really how to go about it! He attempted to communicate this very feeling with Liam. They were sitting before a spitting stove in a hut on the Iron Crossing. Sleet freckled the windows.

Liam, he said, you are like my father, and when I'm near you, I don't know, but it seems like you have a centring in you, like you're part of directions north south east west and, therefore, known. Safe, in part, is what I mean. And then he said, Did you ever glue little strips of felt inside the case of a walnut?

Liam had never done this, never done anything remotely like it. Even so, he shared the rimu bench in front of the spitting stove, and he asked, Is this what you know about, Randall? You know about little things and how to sigh at precisely the right moment, don't you? And your eyelashes—well, they look like they're hiding you.

Randall—his name had quite escaped him until that moment—sat there on the rimu bench beside Liam and he felt as if the hut on the Iron Crossing were crowded with flowers. Hundreds and thousands of creamy bouquets of, say, Early Cheer. But in the morning Liam was up first and polishing the barrel of his rifle with a blue cloth made for that purpose. And then he shouted about bacon and he shouted that he hoped Randall didn't mind a foot of snow because that's what had happened overnight.

*

During this time, but also after this time, Randall renamed himself. He began by calling himself Lamont, but the woman he was dating said she hated that name, said it made her lose respect for him and never want to fuck him ever again. So he went with Charles, which Liam shortened to Chaz. This worked. Sometimes it seemed like it worked very well.

Chaz would be sitting or standing in a room of men—*boys*, they called themselves—most of them Liam's friends but some of them strangers, and some of them—when he looked more closely—not really men or boys at all, but merely statuettes in baseball caps. On these occasions the lights would flicker, or his mind would flicker in a familiar way as he stood near an unlit fireplace, ingesting, ingesting, ingesting: *crackers and cake and wine and smoke and all of these words*.

Coarse and heavy words, like chewing thicker and thicker cardboard and then, home alone, pulling the cardboard from your mouth, yanking it the wrong way up the oesophagus and discovering that it was not cardboard at all, but canvas or oilskin or words written on the trimmed scraps of green lino from the floor of a hallway in a house that was razed, the whole site then levelled, the beeches felled, the stream redirected, the hills shorn, and the sky over all of it wiped away like the fog on a toilet mirror.

When this happened—*if* this happened—Chaz would rush outside and mumble something at the sky's old wound of starlight. Mumble something he didn't remember or would refuse to remember. Then he would return to his bed and collapse and think how wrong he had his own name—how could he ever find it when he didn't know what the hell he was even freakin called?

But the next time this incident befell him, it seemed utterly fresh.

The stars, for instance, didn't recall a word.

*

Chaz was Frederic when Frances and he married, had babies, slogged, crunched, plotted, pirouetted, held each other sometimes even when they were enraged, and, during all of it, never once stood on a stage or at a podium and spoke of whatever it was Frederic had once thought must be said. What they did was to grow heads of grey hair and wash the days from their skin until they were standing shin deep in the brittle bits of so many cast-off years.

How did this happen? they asked the children, but the children were gone.

*

There were delayed flights, redundancies, a second oven, a second refrigerator, a third washing machine, though to be fair the first ones had been on their last legs. Cobwebs draped in the doorways, but not cobwebs like the cobwebs they'd known from their youth.

It was the melting glass of the single panes in their ancient windows, a glazier said.

No, it was the film on their eyes, a master of fishes told them.

No, it was the season. Or the artificial vanilla in the biscotti.

Anyway, it was ordinary, two withered flowers in a vase.

*

Do you remember when Jeremy went skidding on the lawn and embedded that two-pronged nail into his knee and refused to cry for hours in A&E until after the doctor who was an acquaintance of ours pried it out and how—then and only then—we took him in our arms and, oh, how he wept? How later that night in his own bed and well medicated, he asked about it.

Out of nowhere, he asked if they'd seen it.

What I was chasing when I skidded on the lawn, he said. *Do you remember?*

They were sorry. They'd been busy. They hadn't seen a thing.

*

Do you remember later still in our own bed with the girl asleep in the next room dreaming of wings, and of silk armour, and of her own accent in the mouth of mannequin, how the two of us at the end of that day lay there still without one part of our bodies touching? After hours of this—at least it felt like hours—do you remember that one of us said we guessed it was all more complicated than we'd thought, and how this one idea in the air was like a jar of moths had been opened and the moths hung over our heads and then sprinkled softly down onto our bodies until our joints went hot and there in the sadness of that room we found each other again?

Yes, she said, I remember.

And then, whoosh, it happened again.

*

Suddenly the whole world was seeking.

You could catch glimpses of their searches, first on your TV, then on your phone, and then everywhere you looked—you'd see a flash, like the interior of a historical ship cabin or a Latin word in a numbered diagram. Though it's hard to imagine now, people stowed butterfly nets in their cars.

Everyone asked you questions, and you typed small, witty answers which, later, didn't read the way you remembered. Or maybe you simply forgot what you'd written, and then you'd be surprised and half embarrassed when you found the packaging for a butterfly net under the passenger seat of your own car.

So many others, all out there hunting. Liam was hunting, for instance, and all the old mates from those days were hunting. Frances, whom it turned out was friends with the girl who had hated the name Lamont, spent long weekends on the case. The girl who had dreamt of wings and her accent in the mouth of a mannequin was now called Terrance, and he was the only one you knew who was absolutely certain he'd found it, but when you went to his shitty cold flat in Petone he was lying under a mountain of duvets and all you did was listen to the rise and fall of his breath the same as you'd done so many times before.

★

Right around the time Frederic had the second-hand blond wood cabinet delivered up the sixty-six steps, you stopped seeing anything about it online. Or, if you did, it was only a rant (opposed, of course). Simply put, it had been all wrong and it was fabulously glorious that we were past it forever. What came next were overflowing fountains of words. Words like small chocolates or like the panes of a disco ball or like a satchel of thimbles that jingled when you walked.

Frederic placed one small porcelain item beside another small porcelain item in the second-hand blond wood cabinet, and this occupied him ever so completely for most of this era. If the children visited, they would talk about the rain, though they had never wanted to talk about the weather as children. There were new causes, which, it turned out, were very, very old causes that the people between new and old had, to their detriment, spurned.

But it was worse than that, wasn't it?

Much worse, for it turned out that all the people in the room of flickering light were warlocks who practised the vilest of magic. Frederic, it turned out, had been of their order, though inside he'd felt very much as if he was a good warlock practising just the right sort of magic.

Sometimes in this period you would, in fact, find Liam speaking at a podium. If you squinted your eyes, Frederic told Frances, when Liam spoke you could see something of the old boy in the flesh of his upper cheeks just above the dimples. A certain hue of skin that came close to what they'd seen all over the ground at dawn in the hut of the Iron Crossing when it might have been true that they were not at all lost, as Frederic had ardently believed they were at the time.

★

Then it passed out of consideration. People were marching, this is what mattered. The sand was all settling on the short shelves that tapered off into the sea, and this is what mattered. Plus, the children lived in such faraway places it was like they had moved out of the shared world and were now living out their lives in entirely new but vigilantly curated and stunningly bright universes.

Like living in dioramas, Frances said.

Yes, exactly like that, Frederic said. Like dioramas of Ancient Rome or the pre-European contact mound cities of the North American Midwest, or the layers of sediment in the earth, or the cutaway burrow of a muskrat or the strata of a river that had since changed its course and eaten all the mountains, swallowing them whole and then, with their life force gurgling inside, had sung a very quiet song.

No one had heard the song before, and yet we all knew the words.

★

I miss it, he said.
I know you do.

★

But after this—
After *life*, you mean?
I suppose I do.

★

A space so large it is no longer really a space: this is where everyone was housed. It was neither cold nor especially warm. Daylight occurred in the squares of windows so very high above. Panes of light that seemed so pure and so distant it was hard to believe in them at all. The panes of light in our hands, conversely, required no belief whatsoever.

Hosts of us walked. Not looking, just moving. A herd in motion. One peeled off and sat down beside a figure in the half light. One thing was for sure—no one wanted to hear the story about stone soup, not ever again! We were walking, tides and currents of us headed in opposite directions, relying on the flashlight feature of our phones to see.

Who's over there? Is it Liam?

No, I don't think so.

Have you seen this face or seen that face?

Perhaps someone had seen the face or a sought-after item but they could never find it again, even after searching in the most advanced engines the world had ever known.

★

What were you thinking of?

Of flowers, he said. The bright white petal of daisies. Long necks of the irises.

Little bloody wombs of roses?

★

One morning he finds he is able to retrace his steps: Frederic to Chaz to Charlie to Lamont to Randall, the breadcrumbs leading to the window of a little room. He knows the smell of this room because it is mostly his own smell. Balls of crumpled paper on the floor, and when he unwraps the crumpled paper, he knows he will discover the answers he hadn't known were answers at the time.

In the room are a desk, a mirror, a window. No door. A mound of pelts beside the desk—muskrat and badger and possum—and an implausibly cute vest finely sewn from the white fur of a dog who died forty years before.

There had been a time when Frances said something. She'd said, *Did you ever wonder*—but it went no further than that.

If only, though.

Maybe that was all he'd been looking for in the first place.

Terrance sent a letter from a cold place and signed his name with a flourish, in case maybe they forgot and called him the name they had invented while he sloshed about inside of his mother, a little snowboy who they thought was a snowgirl, but whom they both knew was made of nothing but snow. This happened long ago beside the stream before it wandered off, trailing fossils and carports and coming into its own at the long-appointed moment.

★

On the desk, set in the centre beside a pencil and a blank sheet of paper, sits the half shell of walnut lined in blue felt, quite imperfectly glued. Blobs of glue have smooshed out from under the edges of the felt. Even so, he knows it for a pocket of daylight with no cloud.

Or for a featherbed.

Or for the skull of a goose, cleaned and well lacquered.

The walnut is also a casket. A casket that is not now occupied and will never be occupied, not with Frederic present. But if he peers ever so closely inside the shell he can see an indentation. The shape where a body slept before it rose and stretched and walked right through the wall of this room into the supple and unrepentant world.

MICHAEL HALL

View Near the Western Drain

Nothing but drifting clouds—a volcano sky.
The plain's hedge-less paddocks, too.

Notice the moon-like troughs that sit between
Them. Like fenced Jupiter's—all alone.

Sometimes a cow slowly comes, dips
Her muzzle; lifts, dripping—redistributing

The reflections. Thinks briefly, perhaps
Beyond her calf-grief, her fulling stomachs.

How she has led a quiet, half-forgotten life.
I have had no great epiphany either.

MADDIE BALLARD

Little Colonial

When you cross the border, they take you straight to a hotel off the Auckland motorway. You sign your forms with a sanitised pen. Two nurses in sci-fi PPE come to take your temperature each morning; they ask you how you are and listen for your answer. You ask them back and you're listening too. With the breakfast delivered every morning in a brown paper bag there are three feijoas. You have not had a feijoa in two years and they taste impossibly delicious: floral, tart, faintly soapy.

★

They start appearing in March, these hard green fruits—zeppelin-shaped, bumpy-skinned, one end bearing a tight, private stem resembling a half-popped corn kernel. There are several different types of feijoa, also known as the pineapple guava or guavasteen. Big soft feijoas, jellied with juice. Feijoas where there is more of the gritty outer flesh than the wobbly inner. Small feijoas the size of a walnut. Bruised feijoas, feijoas with starched hard scars. Some years you cut into a bucketful and each fruit has a guava moth larva in it, a wriggling brown comma on your spoon. Most feijoas have four or five lobes of flesh. Sometimes there are six or seven lobes; on rare occasions eight. When you cut a feijoa in half, the lobes look like an asterisk in bobbly 1970s font. Each fruit offers only two mouthfuls, the flesh of each half perfectly shaped for a spoon.

★

Your first day outside, you wake in a house you have known all your life. Everything is the same here: the salt air, the bookshelves, the garden of feijoa trees. But the city feels precariously spacious as you walk to the bus stop, like a jacket that doesn't fit anymore. You notice the flat vowels of every passing voice. There's a *Herald* blowing around inside the bin. It's impossible to savour or understand the bus ride you take, let alone the hour you spend wandering around town, hungry for faces. You cannot believe how many people there are in Auckland, filling the CBD with their footsteps and vape smoke.

★

Feijoas picked straight off the tree have a faint bluish-white cast on the skin, a ghostliness soon dissolved by your hands. This blue-white cast has completely disappeared by the time feijoas hit the supermarket, although it can still be spotted at the local veggie market. Its presence in somebody's fruit bowl is how you know they have a source.

You need a source, everybody says. You can't go buying them at Countdown, that's a bloody outrage. Everybody knows somebody with a feijoa tree; or, everybody knows a feijoa tree that hangs over a fence. People take their sources very seriously. All through autumn, in cafés, offices, libraries, you can witness the handover of lidless ice-cream containers and bulging supermarket tote bags. Outside certain houses, sagging cardboard boxes proffer the back yard's bounty: FEIJOAS FREE TO A GOOD HOME. For three months of the year there are only two types of household: feijoa sources and feijoa hunters. The perfume of feijoas hangs everywhere, far from any tree.

⋆

It has always been hard to get a job but now is a particularly inadvisable time to be unemployed. The dad of one of your friends, forty years' experience as a travel agent, has started stacking supermarket shelves. Your aunt, long-time employee of Air New Zealand, is now a part-time medical receptionist. You remember the last time you were writing cover letters, at the same desk where you finished your thesis. You didn't need to worry then, but you didn't know that.

You find yourself with hours to look slowly at everything, which doesn't feel like something you should complain about. You listen to the kōwhai outside your window, loud with tūī each dusk and dawn. You run your body to something far from softness. You read things you've been putting off for a while; you make focaccia, waiting out its long slow rise. You spend time baking with your mother. It is the tail end of autumn and she is trying to use up the last feijoas. Feijoa crumble. Feijoa ice-cream. The newspapers are running the *Edmonds Cookery Book* recipe for feijoa chutney again. No guava moth this year but a lot of small fruit, fiddly to shell. You help her shell them.

⋆

The trees fruit in profusion right until the end of June. If you have a tree, you are actively trying to get rid of feijoas. If you have a tree, you are filling two buckets a day with fallen fruit, scooping their inners and freezing them in big Snap Lock bags. You are pressing old shoeboxes on friends and family—who have been asking since February.

People start tossing around the word 'glut'. The compost bin is one heaving green wave of shells. You are participating in a national sport never seen in public, one of hundreds of thousands of households sitting down to eat six to eight feijoas with breakfast, the fruits split and spooned onto yoghurt and muesli. All that fibre: bowel health has never been better. What will we do with all these feijoas? people say to each other in mock despair. The fruit is rotting all over the lawn in brown decadence, stray specimens popped under the wheels of the car as it comes up the drive. It is not a real question: we wait all year for this.

*

When they weighed your suitcase at the airport it was under the limit. Your life was lighter than expected: you held the lonely thought close all through the flight. You find it easier and easier to pack up, to divest. Eventually you start house-sitting, living in strangers' landscapes. All their animals ask you for love, rolling over to have their soft bellies touched.

You look after a border collie in Westmere—an artist's house, with chickens scratching around the perimeter. You look after a two-week-old calf in the Far North, a toffee-coloured shape in a paddock. You look after a labrador in Mount Eden that lays one pleading paw on your lap when you stop petting her. The gardens are full of feijoa trees, the fruit now vanished. They have a waving Mediterranean look in the back yard, at odds with the rusting lawnmower and the bottle of Wet'n'Forget.

*

Feijoas are native to South America: pockets of Brazil, Uruguay, Argentina and Paraguay. Archaeologists believe the indigenous inhabitants of what is now called Santa Catarina, Brazil, were probably the first people to eat feijoas, sometime after they arrived in the area 4500 years ago.

Feijoas were first made known in the West by German botanist Friedrich Sellow, who collected them in the 1820s while exploring Brazil and Uruguay on the back of a mule. His actions were part of the nineteenth-century project of collecting specimens and bringing them back to the European 'centre'.

The feijoa was named by another nineteenth-century German botanist, Ernst Berger. Its scientific name, Feijoa sellowiana, combines the names of Sellow and a Brazilian naturalist called João da Silva Feijó. To name something, as Jamaica Kincaid has written, is to possess it. '[T]hese new plants from far away, like the people from far away, had no history, no names, and so they could be given names.' I cannot find the original indigenous name for the feijoa anywhere.

It is unclear how the feijoa came to Aotearoa. What we know for certain is that feijoas began to be widely grown here from the 1920s. What we know for certain is that feijoas are an introduced species.

Eventually new varieties were cultivated here. Some were given Māori names: kākāpō, pounamu, kākāriki.

Aotearoa is now one of the largest feijoa producers in the world.

*

You cannot tell anybody exactly what it was like, elsewhere. Sometimes you are unsure it happened: the days and nights spent inside one room; the tiny park nearby soon exhausted from every angle; Boris Johnson babbling on the news; the weeks of empty shelves; the streets of people on balconies, clapping for the NHS. There were thousands of cases in your borough, an area less than half the size of Waiheke Island. You saw a grey-faced woman across the street brought out of her house on a stretcher. You read about the doctor suicides, the makeshift morgues not ten Tube stops away. Your body has not forgotten, but nobody wants to hear what it was like.

*

In England, feijoas are not widely grown and cannot be found in any old supermarket. The climate is all wrong: too cold. Feijoa trees need a few days of frost, but not too many, to fruit well. They do not like extended periods of heat, or heavy wind, or excessive shade. There are Reddit threads dedicated to where you can source feijoas if you live in the UK. Many of the comments are from New Zealanders trying to grow trees away from home: Carla from Waikato, Bob and Niamh from Te Aroha. *Do we need a hothouse?* they ask. *Has anyone tried growing in Shropshire? Would they flourish?*

Others report their modest successes. *Three fruit this year, a bit small but they taste good. Frost got our trees but couple of flowers. Probably easier to fly home.* You can buy a single feijoa for £1.50 at the peak of the season, or import them from overseas for more—but it's a risky game. Feijoas bruise easily so they don't transport well. They have already survived the big migration from South America; now they have new roots.

*

It was the classic OE, everybody said. Kiwis in London. There's a Facebook group: New Zealanders get together for Waitangi Day, dress up as Paula Bennett and jars of Marmite. *Little colonials returning to the mothership*, that's what one of your friends' mothers called it. A rite of passage. *A middle-class Pākehā rite of passage*, you thought.

But you had not moved to London to meet other New Zealanders. You had not moved to order endless pints at the local Wetherspoons, or live in Clapham, or work a marketing job and spend your pounds on summer weekends in Croatia. You had not intended to live in London at all. You had moved to England to study, then stayed on after the degree ended. It was, for you, quite a terrible place to live. You had a time-limited visa and a postgraduate arts degree, and nobody wanted to hire you.

When you were eventually hired, it was by a media company that paid you a salary below the living wage. You left home before it was light. The rain fell on your head. You learnt to write news stories from press releases. You learnt to telephone industry experts for comment, to hold your breath while their clipped receptionists connected you. You studied English defamation law and learnt to record everything someone said. You forgot the conventions of Chicago-style academic referencing, and the lines you loved in *The Waste Land*, and the reason you'd come to England at all.

Your New Zealand accent interested no one, nor the fact that the English you spoke so crisply, earned your livelihood in, was not the native language of the country you were from. Such fine distinctions were irrelevant. One night at the pub a table of men pulled the corners of their eyes at you and shouted *KONICHIWA* so brazenly you were almost impressed. You were so poor, and so overeducated nobody would believe it. You bought your fresh produce at Aldi, where it was sold in cheap, scentless heaps: concussed apples, winter berries in plastic. No kūmara, no kiwifruit, no feijoas.

★

In Britain, the fruit of national fascination is rhubarb. Specifically, there's a fetish for bright pink forced rhubarb, which appears in shops in January. People particularly love the combination of rhubarb and custard—partly for the drama of the colours together, partly for the sweet–sour pairing, partly, admit it, for the nursery sound of the words. Throughout late winter and early spring rhubarb and custard appears on every menu: nutmeg-speckled custard tart with ruby stalks in syrup; pale pink rhubarb and custard gelato; rhubarb and custard fizz; stained-glass lozenges half pink and half yellow. Like feijoas, forced rhubarb is high in pectin and often preserved in jam or jelly form. Unlike feijoas, it looks beautiful in the jar.

*

Despite choosing to leave, you miss London. You miss the buildings rippling in their evening best under Vauxhall Bridge, as if the river were dreaming of them. You miss choir rehearsal in the sixteenth-century cathedral; the spaniels that enquired after your lunch in Brockwell Park; your tiny London Christmas tree, luminous with dried orange slices. The men in fishnets sashaying through Shoreditch at 9am. The twenty weddings' worth of peonies on Columbia Road for the first weekend in spring. The KitKats shelved in the biscuit aisle at Sainsbury's; even the vomit patterning the Sunday morning streets. You could go on and on, never quite saying everything—but even now the details are slipping away. Pretty soon almost all of it will be gone: the kitsch, the luscious, the live.

*

Rhubarb is native to Siberia and China; Marco Polo is credited with introducing it to Europe. Originally valued for its medicinal qualities, and used particularly as a laxative, it was a hot commodity for several centuries. For a period in the seventeenth century, rhubarb was three times more expensive than opium in England, where it was not grown until the 1700s.

Rhubarb came into culinary use in Britain in the early nineteenth century, as sugar became more readily available—an availability directly linked to the transatlantic slave trade.

Forced rhubarb is grown in the dark and harvested by candlelight. Its pale raspberry colour results from denying the plant sunlight, meaning chlorophyll cannot develop. Because the plant is so desperate for light, it grows faster than regular rhubarb. It also tastes sweeter. The forcing method was discovered accidentally and means rhubarb can be produced outside of its regular season.

Rhubarb does not fruit in profusion. It does not hang over fences, tangle in the teeth of lawnmowers, populate kerb-side FREE TO A GOOD HOME boxes, or change hands at the library.

Like the feijoa, rhubarb is an introduced species.

*

Perhaps, you think, eating a mint Trumpet outside the Maungaturoto Four Square, the street smelling of New Zealand rain, it was a fair exchange. Here you are eating ice-cream, after all, in a place where you can see open countryside and harakeke. You could drive to the ocean in minutes. You'll eat kūmara tonight. Mostly, the thingness of things seems much more inherent here. Pak'n'Save is the archetypal supermarket. The chorus line of feijoa trees down the side of the house are The Trees. You know all about bush walks and dollar lolly bags from the dairy, and the volcanoes of Tāmaki waving at one another high up above the city, and white cataracts of sea foam breaking over black sand, and where to buy coffee, and how to greet every single person you meet. You were made of these things and now you know it.

You will know it for a while—how disgustingly lucky you are, always have been. You will keep telling people how nice it is to be home for several months. You will notice every plant, every bird, native or otherwise. Then slowly, almost without your noticing, you'll stop listening to the tūī. You'll find a job of some sort and start flatting again. The feijoa trees will issue their red flowers in spring, resembling pōhutukawa, then shed them in summer. There will be other seasons, other fruits. There will be traffic and bad weather and recreational complaining, and life will become Life: you'll forget it's a variant. As is natural and terrible, your island of knowledge will be subsumed in the tide of everything else.

FIONA KIDMAN

Red River Valley

You may think this is another
nostalgic poem about dancing
when young
though who can forget that once
one's feet could fly
circling to their left and to their right:
rather, it's a poem written
in old age about the valley
that stretches ahead roof top by roof top
beneath the hillside, unchanged
in fifty years and the way
each summer around
Christmas it fills
with sumptuous rich scarlet
abundant crimson, adjectivise it how
ever you like, or just say red, red
pōhutukawa trees clouds of fire burst
raining spiny needles
like embers, rivers of fire, puddles
of sunset on the pavements
between houses lying in that valley
below *may you never forget those sweet hours
ta dum tadum ta dum*
appeasing my blood red
greedy heart with the promise
of another year.

ROSE WHITAU

Birth

That first night of you and I:
The Entities, Mitosis of the Universe—

I stalked your breath,
as it rose and fell in empires,
        there, next to me

I missed you, one hand on my belly
in confusion of twoness,

of worlds in orbit

CHRIS HOLDAWAY

Paorae

    If only pen and ink make a lost land—
Memory's tracts dotted with directions of the wind
—seaward traditions all cousins to erosion cropped
In the very waves of priestly journalism. To see all
Time in the spray eaten at by the equal natures
Of voyages and invocations to encroach; the virtue
Of internecine wars the blue backdrop to history
That sets a precedent for all trance-like states.
Every day we lose sight of esoteric meaning in ex
-change for salt flats and Corinthian downpipes for
Even things celestial are derived of political affairs.
Are we not all the offspring of meteorological ideas
Or the genealogical descent to everlasting rest? O
Solar pastoral; fired tides; our animal pursuits
Both the arcane knowledge and what occludes it.
I say the darkness on water is made in the sky as
Bush in burning soil flows to sea—the breakwinds
Of ceremony place fortifications in what we assume
To be the distance on the holy writ of islands in far
Too translated a place. For it was not proper to use
Ordinary words to draw parallels.

    A riot of wind and sun so I lose my head
Like the nearest stand of trees—every moment a
Body double with a secret deeper than any death.
From all fossilised rivermouths erosion builds
A new world: a golden age of heavy metals settling
Your blood like rainwater; contemplating infinity
From the beach in any silicate instrument. All light

Goes to waste if not through stained glass—the
Cottage industry of the future at once heavy and
Aglow with horizons. Our twin miracles electricity
And root crops depend on loose soils dragged back
From the underworld. Our antiquated notions of
Utopia may yet refuse a flaxen Atlantis and so over
-turn the earth. For all the perfection of historical
Records in the sky knowledge should risk being
Destroyed by flood or fire if we are to reclaim
The antediluvian days when forests were always
Alight. No bead of satellites truly traces mudflats
Gone beneath the waves; the poetry of the future is
Not enough to forever cross the bridge like what
Preceded darkness.

PHOEBE WRIGHT

The Great Alpine Highwire Act

Before the accident, neither the little family in the sunny, slopy port town nor their neighbour knew that what they had was Arcadia. Though perhaps little Fliss knew. When she was still Fliss: a warm tumble of fluffed braids, unbounded ideas and eccentric fears. Before she became Felicity: a Stuff.co.nz headline, a cautionary tale.

The week the family moved in, Will, Fliss's father, walked in on Bracken, the neighbour, masturbating. Hana, Fliss's mother, had baked sourdough. She wanted them to introduce themselves to the neighbours, which seemed unnecessarily formal to Will. Then Hana developed a sore throat, so Will took the bread over alone. He knocked on the open door, called out, heard faint music. It was completely unlike him to enter uninvited, yet he did.

Bracken was lying on the couch. A fraying, silky, plum-coloured kaftan slipped over his thigh. Beneath it, his hand worked and a buried vibrator buzzed. Bracken's generous eyelashes fluttered; his back arched over the squishy arm of the couch. On the other arm sat a black cat that looked smugly at Will, who turned and ran and buried the bread in the garden.

Bracken was born Samuel and renamed himself Rārahu at a festival when he was twenty, then when he was told it was appropriation, he changed it to the English plant name, claiming the change had always been mainly about his affinity for the species, which his friends didn't believe.

Fliss befriended the now thirty-five-year-old jack of all trades through the holes in the fence. When she asked him if she could come over to see his talking cats and glowing strawberries, Bracken knocked on his neighbours' front door to introduce himself and ask if Will and Hana would like their daughter to learn some gardening with him, it being no trouble. The verdict was as long as she stayed in sight of her own kitchen window. The properties were sloped so you could see most of Bracken's garden from their kitchen window. So I can call Fliss home easily, Hana quickly added, seeing Bracken's jaw shift a little.

Will and Hana watched through the kitchen window as Bracken taught their daughter how to pinch the laterals from tomato plants. Hana smiled and murmured, Look at her.

Yup, it takes a village, Will said. He never told her about walking in on Bracken.

*

That summer, Fliss made an elaborate shelter of sticks against the leaning fence under Bracken's grapevine, with a mosaic floor of dirt-pressed beer caps and wine lids, which Bracken saved for her every time he drank with his friends. Willow-woven dreamcatchers sprouted from trees. They made tiny bonsai gardens in Indian takeaway boxes full of dirt with sprigs of native shrubs, colourful pebbles and matchstick fences. Magic crackled at Fliss's earth-grubbed fingertips.

Fliss pressed her face to her bedroom window when Bracken's friends traipsed down the steps to his house. Hana called them a motley crew but Fliss loved them: the ones with large breasts and impressive whiskers; the women who wore long flowing dresses and their long hair loose, in contrast to her mother's high ponytails and alternating office wear and activewear. Once, Fliss snuck out and sat on Bracken's doorstep to listen to the drunken, glorious guitar and waiata. She sat in rapture amongst the piled shoes: near-broken Warehouse jandals, several pairs of identical Birkenstocks worn well down into the cork, crusty skate shoes, and purple velvety pumps the texture of a cat's nose. Bracken's cats, Jacinda and Winston, sniffed the shoes with a raptured, thorough sensuality.

*

Hana fretted over the weed smoke and cat shit Fliss might encounter in Bracken's garden. But, as she and Will repeated to each other, neither of them could teach Fliss about growing things. And, they said, it was probably good for her to have relationships with animals, though it was abhorrent that Bracken kept outdoor cats while native bird and gecko populations fell to a new bloodied low each summer. Hana chased Jacinda and Winston from their own property with great hissing conviction and a broom. She tried to get Fliss to do the same for the sake of her daughter's beloved skinks and pīwakawaka, which Will photographed with his work camera. But Fliss could not bear the

LANDFALL 247

Dedicated to the memory of Vincent O'Sullivan,
1937—2024

May 2024

Editor Lynley Edmeades

Reviews Editor David Eggleton
Founding Editor Charles Brasch (1909–1973)

Cover: Kate van der Drift, *Apples (after Gabrielle)*, 2023, archival pigment print, 750 x 1000mm.

Published with the assistance of Creative New Zealand.

OTAGO UNIVERSITY PRESS

CONTENTS

- 4   Landfall Young Writers' Essay Competition 2024 Judge's Report, *Lynley Edmeades*
- 6   Fourteen Robyns, *Emma Hughes*
- 10   The Drunken Hedge, *Nick Ascroft*
- 12   In-flight (lovers) of Bristol Street, St Albans, *Ariana Tikao*
- 13   The Case of the Walnut, *Thom Conroy*
- 21   View Near the Western Drain, *Michael Hall*
- 22   Little Colonial, *Maddie Ballard*
- 29   Red River Valley, *Fiona Kidman*
- 30   Birth, *Rose Whitau*
- 31   Paorae, *Chris Holdaway*
- 33   The Great Alpine Highwire Act, *Phoebe Wright*
- 39   Shell Fighting in the Pacific, *Federico Monsalve*
- 40   Baking, *Michelle Elvy*
- 41   Seeing Things, *Lucinda Birch*
- 45   Right Now: A Triolet, *Harry Ricketts*
- 46   art versus the world, *Chris Tse*
- 48   Resort, *Mark Edgecombe*
- 49   with friends like these, *Zephyr Zhang 张挚*
- 50   The End Was Wide Open, *James Pasley*
- 58   Yoke, *Nicholas Wright*
- 59   painting, *Vaughan Rapatahana*
- 61   Self-driving Cars, *Nicola Andrews*
- 62   Mistranslation, *Emma Neale*
- 63   The Children, *Greg Judkins*
- 64   ART PORTFOLIO *Kate van der Drift*
- 73   A Bit of a Mess, *James O'Sullivan*
- 77   Papering, *Nicola Thorstensen*
- 79   First Charge, *Chris Cantillon*
- 80   Sweetie, *Michelle Duff*
- 85   The Plastisphere, *David Eggleton*
- 86   Underneath it All, *Kristin Kelly*
- 92   Stars on Every Lemon Tree, *Medb Charleton*
- 93   My Mother's Skin, *Wes Lee*
- 94   Playing with Dolls, *Kit Willett*

95 trees, *Brett Cross*
96 ART PORTFOLIO *Ayesha Green*
105 Make Horse Beach, Moloka'i, *Kirby Wright*
106 Denial, *Lorraine Carmody*
112 Petroglyph, *Craig Foltz*
114 The Tōtara at 14 Stanley, *Connie Buchanan*
119 I was born crooked, *Zoë Meager*
120 all our warmth and colour, *Rebecca Ball*
121 The best bird for your return, *Claire Orchard*
122 The Lovely Boys, *Scott Menzies*
126 Mudlarking, *Mikaela Nyman*
128 below the graft, *Nathaniel Calhoun*
129 Geraniums, *Cindy Botha*
130 A singer returns, *Harvey Molloy*

MAKING SPACE: IN COLLABORATION WITH RMIT UNIVERSITY'S non/fictionLab
132 THE EARTH WILL BE FINE, *Mia-Francesca Jones & Lauren Vargo* / 143 RE-POEMING AS A PRACTICE OF MAKING SPACE FOR ALTERNATIVE DOCUMENTARY APPROACHES, *Airini Beautrais & Jessica L. Wilkinson* / 157 AFFIDAMENTO: THE MAKING OF A SHARED WRITTEN ROOM, *Amy Brown & Joan Fleming*

THE LANDFALL REVIEW
170 Landfall Review Online: Books recently reviewed / 171 IAN WEDDE on *Gordon Walters* by Francis Pound / 176 DAVID HERKT on *The Book Collector: Reading and living with literature* by Tony Eyre / 180 SIMONE OETTLI on *Tangi: The 50th anniversary edition* by Witi Ihimaera / 183 BRONWYN WYLIE-GIBB on *Bird Life* by Anna Smaill / 187 HELENE WONG on *Backwaters* by Emma Ling Sidnam / 190 IAIN SHARP on *Rapture: An anthology of performance poetry from Aotearoa New Zealand* edited by Carrie Rudzinski and Grace Iwashita-Taylor, and *Remember Me: Poems to learn by heart from Aotearoa New Zealand* edited by Anne Kennedy

202 CONTRIBUTORS
208 LANDFALL BACKPAGE *Pat Kraus*

LYNLEY EDMEADES

Landfall Young Writers' Essay Competition 2024 Judge's Report

The winning writers of this year's essay competition are wise to our shortcomings: as we devise strategies to counter the various global issues on our doorstep, a younger generation continues to show us the consequences of our not-quite-getting-around-to-it. Why the gratuitous bureaucracy and petty politics when people in Gaza are dying in droves? Who cares if landlords don't get a tax break if there are still people without a home? Why does it matter who owns the rainforest if it's on fire? The questions and concerns of this year's essays go a long way in showing up the immense and increasing absurdity of some of our so-called 'mature' behaviour. As we age, we become more and more inured to the banality of evil, to use Hannah Arendt's words; the messages of these young writers are a gift to help us see this.

    The winner of this year's competition, 'Fourteen Robyns' by **Emma Hughes**, puts a spotlight on austerity and bureaucracy. It recounts the story of a young woman's visit to Family Planning but withholds the reason why she is there in the first place. Of course, one doesn't have to reach too far to imagine why she might be there, but the attention of the protagonist towards her surroundings provides a kind of portrait of the setting and its inhabitants, subtly asking: *why does it have to be like this?* It shows immense skill as a writer to say so little about oneself, to extol any opinions or explicitly state 'what' the essay is about, particularly in the 'personal essay' space (that so often lends itself to confessional or didactic tones). In the awkward liminality of the waiting room, we take in all that Hughes notices: the effusive receptionist, a heavily pregnant patient, a tired mother with a toddler, a mother with her teenage daughter, a woman with a black eye and a limp. There is something of the anthropologist's eye here, a gaze that allows the writer the knowledge that there is a reality bigger than her own. Hughes' observations urge the reader to absorb something of the atmosphere of the place: 'cushions covered confusion this wrought upon Jacinda and Winston, to whom she was a trusted friend.

⋆

One day, too hot to garden or play, Bracken read Fliss a book he had kept from childhood, sitting in her grapevine-shaded hutlet. In the tattered book a girl lived above a pub, and a man who travelled from town to town walking a highwire arrived. He rigged a wire in the courtyard behind the pub where the girl hung sheets. She begged him to teach her, but he said, looking tragic and handsome, No, because once you walk the highwire, you will never be happy on the ground again. Bracken did such an inexplicably Kiwi-bloke accented tragic handsome voice that Fliss snorted fizzy water out her nose and then said, after coughing messily, My face was full of stars just then. Winston lunged to headbutt Bracken on the cheek with vigorous love.

⋆

Bracken helped Will dig away a shelf of earth beneath the family's balcony to be a garden bed for Fliss. Bracken said, We can make sections with stones and different coloured herbs so it forms a picture from above. Maybe a mandala.

Or a highwire walker! said Fliss. Their digging unearthed a rusty waratah from some long-ago fencepost. They tried to remove it but decided, when it wouldn't budge, to wait for rain to soften the soil. But the summer was longer and hotter than any in memory. Rain never came.

⋆

Fliss balanced, arms held out gracefully, along raised kerbs, garden fences, tree branches and, one day, a slackline Bracken tied between two olive trees. Hana saw her daughter stepping onto the thin strap from the window, her hand held by Bracken in those ridiculous Aladdin pants. Hana suddenly remembered Fliss needed a haircut and ended the fun.

Fliss surmised that she would not be allowed to walk the tantalising balcony rail of her house so she never tried it, except once, in the early morning, when her parents were still asleep. Bracken, drinking coffee on the ground amongst his plants, saw her, silhouetted against the gold of the sunrise, hair lifting on the nor'wester. It took his breath away and he muttered to his tomatoes, Your secret's safe with me, kid.

⋆

The night was too hot for Fliss to sleep but her parents were managing: Will snoring back at the whirring fan, which fluttered the pile of half-marked essays on Hana's bedside table. Fliss crept in to study her mother's face, with its black smudges from sweat and makeup, her expression so much softer in sleep. On the balcony, under stars drunk on the hot wind, Fliss saw Bracken's house lit like a paper lantern. Music and sweet smoke drifted over the fence. Fliss thought of the girl in the book, stepping forward onto the wire to meet the melancholic but beautiful man who walked through the sky for a living. She climbed onto the cane chair and then onto the balcony rail.

Will found his child in the morning, lying more still than ever since he first met her, the day he touched her tiny shoulder through Hana's hot belly skin. The only movement now was the wind teasing her hair. The waratah protruded bloodily from her lower back.

Will felt he should lift her off it himself. Carry the skewered little body to her bed, lay her with flowers and Ted and her books. But he could not move, and was still crouching in his dressing gown beside the lemon tree when two line-faced firefighters came to lift Fliss off the waratah. Will thought one of Bracken's cats was sick and moaning somewhere and then realised the noise was coming from his own throat. Hana watched from the balcony and looked away from Fliss only once: to stare across at the curtained window of Bracken's place, where a cat yawned between curtain and glass.

★

When Bracken showed up at the funeral, Hana started shaking and asked her father and brothers to remove him. A non-plussed Bracken was escorted out and told, Sorry mate. Yeah, not sure, but it's probably for the best right now.

★

Casseroles turned up until they didn't. Will and Hana returned to work sooner than their friends thought they should. Hana looked for Fliss in her students' faces but Fliss was nowhere, and wouldn't be, ever again in all the universe. When Hana abruptly stopped going to work, Will nodded numbly. He should probably stay home with her. But then Will picked up the phone when Hana's work friend called and said, Just let her know: the school has cited recent trauma, and the family aren't likely to go down the legal route.

When Will asked Hana what had happened at school, she looked through him.

⋆

While Bracken was away at a festival, Hana broke into his house and found the book about the highwire walker. When she read it, she felt something like the pleasing clunk her lower spine sometimes achieved when she stretched just the right way. Hana took Bracken's book, along with his slackline. Then she grated rat poison into Jacinda and Winston's jellymeat. Bracken came back to find their soft bodies sprawled beside the salad bowl he filled with water for them, which they had licked dry in the desperate thirst of the poison's throes.

One week later, Will knocked on Bracken's door to tell him Hana had been hospitalised. Doctors were talking about a 'psychotic episode'. Will had come home to find her packing, raving, convinced that somewhere in the Alps was a place where if one strung a highwire and walked it, it would become a rift between heaven and hell or our world and the next. If Hana leapt into the rift, she could bring Fliss home. Bracken's book was full of her crazed notes. She believed it to be a code. On a topo map she had circled a range called the Dragon's Teeth.

I'm so sorry about your cats, Will told Bracken. Bracken, numb from crying, didn't react. Are you wearing black for them? Will continued. Bracken was wearing a long black linen kaftan. Will was wearing the same clothes he had been wearing under his dressing gown when Fliss died.

And for Fliss, Bracken said.

You didn't wear it after she died, Will thought.

Bracken sighed. What do you want?

I found these kittens, said Will. Their mum was whelping in a reserve where I was on a shoot. They're in the car. I just thought—

No.

At least come and meet them.

Bracken did, and when he saw the tabby sister and black and white brother asleep in a yin-yang koru, he named them Tusiata and David Seymour. Will came in for a drink and then a smoke. They sat on the couch and watched the kittens explore Bracken's lounge.

⋆

Will visited Hana daily but she was not interested in him, even as her medication began to work and she began to hold rational conversations with her psychologist. Upon her release from hospital she moved into a long-term house-sitting gig in Heathcote. She rigged up Bracken's slackline in her house-sit's back yard, and then a wire. Two months later, at an environmental protest in Cathedral Square, she donned an enlarged version of the tūī costume she had once made for Fliss and walked a wire between two lampposts, flapping balletically.

    The organisers told her she was likely the reason the protest made the news. She walked the wire at actions for climate, water rights, and then a ceasefire in Gaza, in a hijab, holding a paint-bloodied bundle of pillow and wrapped sheets to represent a child. Hana learned tricks of footwork, jumping and twisting and pretending to lose her balance, and she busked with a sign that said All Proceeds to Forest & Bird. A city council representative told her she had to wear a harness as the wires grew higher. She did, and then casually unclipped it the moment she stepped onto the wire.

*

Hana had not spoken to Will in three months when she burst into their old house looking for her camp stove. Will and Bracken were sitting shirtless on the balcony, smoking a bowl and talking about Fliss. Tusiata and David tussled joyously at their feet. The men froze. The cats continued obliviously.

    Hana was unsurprised and unconcerned. She told them she was about to be photographed and filmed on a highwire between two spectacular peaks. She was going to be on some special summer segment of the TV news. The helicopter and film crew were ready to go. But she didn't know if there would be coffee on top of the mountain, and she always drank an expresso shot immediately before wire walking, so she wanted the stove. Hana gave Will and Bracken not a moment's window to speak, though they wouldn't have known what to say.

    Her bluster stopped for a second when she turned in the doorway with the stove in her hands. She looked at them and said, with a beautiful, lit-from-within smile, I'll tell Fliss you both say hello. Then she was gone.

FEDERICO MONSALVE

Shell Fighting in the Pacific

The hermit crab enclosure began to rumble some time before the main tremor, giving the little crustacean just enough time to put its affairs in order. First there was the thing about epistemology, which had to be hunted for in the laundry room and brought out of effacement. Then there was Marie. The lovely Marie with her voluptuous braids who loved nothing more than citrus almonds. She once said: 'Believe me when I tell you ...' and the echoes of that still reverberate, just enough to crumble the weakest of fossilised shells.

MICHELLE ELVY

Baking

Mother pulls the tray from the oven
with the big red mitt because it's hot, very hot,
flips the wee men with their rounded legs and arms
onto the board, pours icing sugar into a bowl.
The kitchen is cosy.

Son says, Can I have one, yum and
I'm doing a report on global warming,
asks, How can I summarise something
so enormous, so *colossal*?
Mother didn't know he knew that word.

Daughter says, Me too, but Mother warns,
They are hot, very hot,
and Son says, I mean the whole
fucking planet's on fire.
Mother's never heard him say that word either

but says to one, Careful, here, use this,
and to the other, Yes, the whole fucking planet.
Son says, So see, I need help, because
I have to write it in a paragraph.
The whole world in a page.

Meanwhile Daughter dollops icing
on the hot hot gingerbread men, three little buttons,
and watches as the white peaks melt away. They're gone,
she says, just like that. And Mother says, too hot,
and Son says, Yeah, just like that.

Too fucking hot.

LUCINDA BIRCH

Seeing Things

Nullabor Desert, South Australia
About fifty kilometres into the Nullabor we turned off the main highway and headed south to the ocean at the bottom of the continent, where the vast desert dropped straight into the brine. The plunging ninety-metre cliffs were striped brown and swooped westward in an unbroken ribbon as far as we could see. It was like standing on the edge of the world.

At the Head of Bight visitor centre we bought tickets to access the boardwalks that zig-zagged down the cliffs to several long platforms held about ten metres above the ocean. The sky was cobalt blue. The sea was turquoise. There were six southern right whales floating close below us, and five of them had calves. The calves zipped and zapped about; they rammed and nudged and bothered their mothers. They suckled and spouted. Occasionally one of the enormous females would roll over and slap at a pesky calf with her round pectoral fin.

Further out in the bay a slab of black erupted from the water: another whale, a split-second Zeppelin. The man on the platform next to us cheered, and so did we.

We watched for hours until our eyes were full, then we drove about twenty kilometres back into the desert to the Nullabor Roadhouse and checked in to the motel. Our room was grey concrete brick with an ochre bathroom and maroon sheets. We had dinner in the small bar crowded with truck drivers, perched on bar stools that creaked and swayed like small ships in a storm. The man next to me was friendly. He had just driven a 1972 Holden Statesman across the Nullabor's Old Road. 'How was that?' I asked. 'Dusty,' he answered.

Later, wrapped in maroon sheets, I lay in bed and thought about the whales, not so far away but submerged. Floating, breathing, sinking. Floating, breathing, sinking. Strange not-fish in the deep watery darkness of the desert.

Port Pirie, South Australia
We stopped at Port Pirie so I could see Shakka the Shark. Shakka was a 5.5-metre great white caught and drowned in snapper nets in a local bay, and now preserved and displayed at the Port Pirie Tourism & Arts Centre. The man behind the information desk was wide eyed and hopping with enthusiasm. 'Yes, she's here! You won't be disappointed!' he said. We paid three dollars each and the man led us down a corridor and unlocked a door. 'Tah dah!' he said. There was Shakka. Or rather, a fibreglass replica of Shakka. The only genuine parts of the shark left were the jaw and rows of teeth. The room was bright green. 'I'll leave you here,' said the man. 'Just let yourselves out when you've finished.' He closed the door behind him. I tried to imagine the huge fibreglass shark alive and swimming in the sea, but the model was too smooth and shiny and, despite its anatomical perfection, it didn't look real at all. I was a little disappointed.

Afterwards we went for a walk over and along Port Pirie Creek, which was as wide as a river, and then we went to the supermarket. The young man at the checkout had blond Hollywood good looks and a deadpan expression. His nametag said GRAY. 'I bet you get called Gary a lot,' said Rob. Gray smiled. 'Are you from out of town?' he asked. 'Where are you going?' 'The Nullabor,' Rob answered. 'My advice is do not under any circumstances pick up any hitchhikers. It's dangerous out there,' Gray said in a monotone. 'Okay,' I said. 'What do you do?' he asked me as he stashed our groceries with beautiful precision. 'I write stories,' I said. 'Can you put me in one of your stories?' Gray asked. 'Sure,' I said.

Geraldton, Western Australia
There was nothing wrong with Geraldton but we didn't feel at ease there. It was a Sunday when we arrived and everything was closed. We'd booked a motel ahead because we were tired and dirty and wanted to sit and look at the sea, but when we arrived we found our ocean-view room looked straight at the neighbour's brick wall.

We drove up a hill overlooking the town to see the memorial to the HMAS *Sydney II*, a ship that had been torpedoed and sunk by a German warship in 1941 in the Indian Ocean. All 645 crew died. The memorial was called the *Dome of Souls*. It was a large rounded cupola made up of 645 stainless steel silver gulls, one gull for each dead sailor's spirit, echoing the old superstition that seagulls are drowned sailors reincarnated. Three months after the sinking of the *Sydney* a life-raft washed up on Christmas Island containing the remains of one of the crew. The corpse had been cooked by the sun and was partially decomposed, stabbed by birds and gnawed by crabs. Despite its lofty beauty and brazen symbolism, the *Dome of Souls* seemed hard-edged and desolate.

We went back to the motel and asked if we could change rooms. We moved to a room with a view of the ocean and two large kitchen chillers next door. We sat and looked at the open grave of the sea and the hefty refrigerators rattled and hummed. That night I couldn't sleep. The noise from the chillers was inconsistent, and louder in the dark. I lay awake and worried about gulls. A cloud of gulls circling over the town, a scavenging of silver gulls pecking the eyes out of dead sailors, the squawking screaming apparitions of everyone ever drowned.

Shark Bay, Western Australia
We tried to go for a swim near the jetty at Monkey Mia but when Rob waded into the water a decent-sized shark swam up fast. Rob danced knees high onto the beach. I laughed. The shark sashayed back and forth in front of us, then flicked its tail and speared away into the deep.

    We drove back towards the highway through pink sand desert which was covered in a sparse carpet of grey shrubby plants with sparky names—acacia, samphire and spinifex. Every so often there'd be a group of sandalwood. Taller twisted scented trees, some of them 300 years old. Arid desert parasites sucking at the roots of the plants that surround them.

    The desert was spacious and light. The sky was washed out and transparent grey. We followed a sign to Eagle Point Bluff Lookout on a whim. We stood on the boardwalk built across the top of the low cliffs and looked out over the vast flat ocean. Shark Bay stretched into the distance, four kilometres of rolling sandbanks covered with wire-weed and ribbon-weed like underwater lawns. It was patterned sea-grass dark green and white-sand aqua. In the light shallows millions of tiny bait fish swarmed and murmurated like water-bound starlings. Six huge sharks cleared paths in the black fish clouds, slicing pulsing shapes into the hordes. One of the sharks was a hammerhead, the shape of its head distinct and strange.

    Later that evening in the supermarket at Carnarvon there was a small girl in the checkout queue in front of us. She was blonde, tanned golden. She wore a yellow spaghetti-strapped top with an enormous live brown moth clinging to the front like a weighty furred brooch. Moths scare me, so I kept my distance.

HARRY RICKETTS

Right Now: A Triolet

for Belinda

Right now, at least, there's still the worry,
though, soon enough, even that will be gone,
transformed to grief and all its carry-on.
Right now, at least, there's still the worry—
and the love—and keeping things slow: to hurry
only speeds up that which cannot be undone.
Right now, at least, there's still the worry,
though, soon enough, even that will be gone.

CHRIS TSE

art versus the world

back then, between what was lost & what was to be found
I lay awake, ready to concede that I,

too, had been a space prone to failing because I persevered
through the world's agonies

without pulling away & grew to accept how they settled
on my skin, which is to say

there was a time when I was very used to the present tense
how it tested my limits

& my reliance on fortune-telling, which felt more convenient
than writing my own future

nowadays, everything I write is an attempt at manifestation
because it's the only control I have

instead of screaming at alarmist headlines or dog whistles
I imagine glitter raining over my head

see that cloud? that cloud looks like Big Gay Energy
making every month Pride Month

I rinsed the last party from my hair & yet it still followed
me across the country to settle on

someone else's kitchen floor—tell-tale glint of dancing in
mesh & harness under neon lights

where everything that has the potential to hurt me lurks
at the door, tongues clicking

knife makes knife-shape & dark makes dark-shape &
in response art makes hope in the shape

of running ahead to pull back the velvet curtain before
the crowd knows to gather with pitchforks

I tell myself we will survive whatever the light touches
because I've seen

what can happen to light when passed through glass
& split into its constituent parts

every surface becomes a witness to its coming out &
its power to change but leave no mark

but tell me if I'm placing too much faith in something
so ordinary, that I should still

keep my camouflage nearby in case the clocks are
turned too far back

to a time when a flickering signifier would attract
a lethal hunger

MARK EDGECOMBE

Resort

Poolside is loungers decked in cobalt squabs.
Poolside is towel-skirts and backwards-facing caps.
Poolside's a Bitter. Poolside's a Gold.
Poolside is Boney M, loud. Yes, poolside is riverside,
it's rivers of Babylonside. Poolside is humming
Lorde's songs. It's a strange land.
Poolside's a luxe made for us. It's
listening in. It's eyeing up. Poolside's
a waitress seeing me seeing her, and smiling.
It's a plastic frangipani behind the ear.
Poolside is Bula! Poolside's Vinaka!
Poolside's the upside that doesn't have a downside.
Poolside is Bendigo and rural New South Wales.
Poolside's last stop before tipping the scales.

But the palms. That line of them
rising over the hotel roof
like licked fingers raised,
their fronds plunging and swaying,
swaying and plunging,
languid compulsive semaphore;
the palms rising on the angle and up,
surfing the stratum the easterly gusts.
Poolside, I watch them,
wish I could be where they are,
the hell out of this resort.
They're in most of the photos I've taken,
perfect for framing horizons and sunsets.
The snaps we resort to for proof we were here.

ZEPHYR ZHANG 张挚

with friends like these

I am house-sitting a fish
it keeps doing this thing where it pretends to be dead
and then looks at me to check if I noticed
my friend tells me it's doing it for attention
I say that doesn't make it any less valid
it's still a call for help

I tell my friend that I'm thinking about donating a kidney
she says why are you telling me this
donating an organ doesn't make you a good person

my friend is telling me about her very long dream
I think about that meeting where the main topic was scheduling another meeting
I think about my colleague telling me the difference between a variegated melon and a non-variegated melon
I tell my friend I think I might have adhd
she says no you don't

on friday night I consider going out
instead I watch the fish breathe
in and out, in and out

JAMES PASLEY

The End Was Wide Open

For the past six weeks Annie has been sleeping with a teacher named Patrick Drury. Twice he has tried to call it an affair. Twice she has considered correcting him. But she likes how he looks when he says it. She likes that he's older than her. That he's recently separated. She likes that he isn't handsome; his hair is thinning; he has narrow shoulders, a weak chin. He also has big eyes and is prone to sudden bursts of joy that—when she is responsible—always makes her feel so happy.

He lives alone in a seaside flat in Devonport that's basically on the sand. His kitchen has a view of Rangitoto. This helps, she thinks. Location always helps. They lie in on the weekends and listen to the sea. Some mornings when it's early and he's making coffee, she goes down to the water. She pulls up her dressing gown, wades in and waits for him. Her favourite part is watching him slowly pad to her. On these mornings it all feels new.

Today she's already dressed—dark skirt, dark shirt, a blazer over the chair. He's still asleep. Naked, he looks lanky and ungainly: a teenager. It's their last day together and he has no idea.

'Pat,' she says. 'We need to go.'

'Sure,' he says, unable to open his eyes.

★

She only turns once before the auction starts. She wants to look at them, to know them, so that later she can imagine who is living in the house and eating under the oak and watching the wind move through the fields.

'It's not too late,' her brother says, beside her.

'Shut up,' she says, looking forward again.

Sam Kroeber, the agent, a man known for waiting in hospice carparks to pick up new clients, crouches to say hello. He is unapologetic. He says whatever comes into his head. The first time they met, a week after her mother died, he asked if he could buy her parents' leather couches.

'All good, darling?' he says now. Nobody used to notice her.

'This feels like a funeral.'

'I guess it kinda is,' he says. 'Except the only thing we offer after is champagne.'

The auction room even looks like the parlour where they had the service: dark wood panelling, high ceiling, chairs in rows, a nervousness about what will happen, *if* anything will happen. The people are all strangers. The only person she really knows is waiting for her outside, parked on yellow lines.

'Good morning, ladies and gentlemen,' Sam Kroeber says from up front.

She remembers that much; the rest is blurry. All that's left is a feeling, the same feeling she had at Rainbow's End—a feeling that envelops her as she closes her eyes and falls and falls, as she waits for it to be over. And then she hears it. The crack of the hammer. That happy voice.

*

The first meal afterwards is cheap and salty and they eat it alone in the park by the ferry. Devonport is quiet, the shops are empty. It's late on a Tuesday morning and the rest of the country is at work, hurrying to finish for the year. Pat called in sick on the way to the auction house.

'It doesn't matter,' he said as he waited for someone to pick up. 'Exams are over.'

He stretches out now, cat-like, relaxed. They are lying on a blanket on the grass and for the first time she has an inkling of regret—he even thought of bringing a blanket.

When he pulls his shirt up to scratch his belly she thinks, relax, you barely know him.

She thought he was being friendly the first time he took her hand. She figured he was going above and beyond the night he took her home after her mother died. She was sure of it even when he started messaging her, asking to see her, telling her he missed catching glimpses of her across the yard. The day he knocked at the back door she began to wonder.

She considers herself an open person, but there were signs—the curl over his forehead, the books and flowers and candles littered through the flat, the mint-green Saab jauntily parked across the driveway, but mostly, really, it was the way he treated her mother with such decency, driving her to the hospital because Annie couldn't. He is so unlike her brothers. It made her think he wouldn't be interested.

'Well,' he says, 'and how does it feel?'

'I don't know,' she says. 'When it happened I felt so light. But I think I've come back down again.'

'Don't worry,' he says. 'That's only natural.'

For the past three years she hasn't had a life. Her weekends were spent with her mother at the family's old farmhouse, her weeks in an office downtown.

Her mother is dead now and her boss doesn't know about the auction. Yesterday she told him she was taking a personal day, tomorrow she will be gone. She hasn't given notice. On her desk she left the oppressive statue her father gave her on her first day and a picture of her family under the oak. She is glad to be rid of them. But she will miss the people—the familiar faces at the coffee shop, at the op shop, most of all on the hotel's top floor, a bar no one knows about, an oasis she hid in every Friday night as she waited for her mother to pick her up and take her back to Kumeu. She is twenty-four years old. She has never left home.

'Is it?' she says.

After they're finished eating they walk along the road by the water, then up North Head through long grass.

He's in teaching mode—panting as he explains how it formed; sweating as he tells her simple stuff, first-year stuff even she remembers, like how there are fifty-three volcanoes across Auckland and how the country sits 'smack bang' on the ring of fire. He's enthusiastic. This is how he talks to his students, how he makes them care. He thinks he and Annie are the same—people with big hearts.

The truth is she doesn't care about anything except for how it makes her feel. The farm was shade and silence and birdsong. Now it is money and freedom and guilt. It'll take her years to admit that's why she is leaving.

He tells her that Lake Taupo was the biggest eruption ever. Smoke was seen in Rome.

'Rome,' he says a second time, turning to look at her. 'Can you believe it?'

'I can,' she says.

She knows most of it already but that almost makes it better. His spiel is like a quiet song in the background, an old song she hasn't heard in years, one she almost forgot.

They climb onto the roof of one of the old cannon emplacements and sit against each other on the concrete. There's nothing comfortable to relax on, no wall to lean against. She wonders how she used to do it. She remembers having sex up here with her first boyfriend all the time. He was a cold fish who, looking back, seemed to hate her. They saw each other for a year and he never once said anything he really thought.

She wonders, how do I tell him? When do I tell him?

★

Annie is finally realising today she's all alone. Her mother's gone and sealed it. Her father died what feels like a long time ago now—just a few weeks after her twenty-first birthday. It wasn't unexpected. He had been under a lot of pressure. It had been the same story her whole life. When he wasn't working he locked himself in an office behind their house down by the water. Who knows what he did in there. By the time she went for a closer look it had been cleaned out and closed off. For a few years her mother kept it shut up, then one day she decided to rent it out. To make a little money, she said.

When Pat showed up to look at it, her mother wasn't sure. 'He's a bit odd,' she said. 'The teacher. How's he going to pay the rent on his salary?'

Annie said, 'What school?'

'That Catholic boys' school in Takapuna, the one with the bad priest.'

'That's just the newspapers,' she said. 'I know a guy who went there and he was all right.'

It has always confused her why he teaches. His mother left when he was a boy. His father sold cars in Oamaru. His brother works in the mines. Pat must have been different when he was young: he captained the rugby team. She can't imagine him giving a rousing speech. They would have lost every single match.

'What are you thinking about?' he says.

'The heat,' she says. 'Since when did it get this hot so early in December?'

Sometimes after sex he tells her about his students. Colourful stories about the dumb, violent things they do. Asthma inhaler burns, compass cuts, fights under the science block. She hears his gravelly voice, sees candles flickering through half-closed eyes. She never really listens and usually forgets what he tells her. But she remembers one story. He told her during a storm about one of his students beating up a kid after the kid told everyone the student had written a love letter to his own sister. His student hadn't known the girl was his sister. Pat was amazed that this brute who spoke in single syllables had written a whole page—and to a stranger.

She opened her eyes when he told her the final line of the letter. 'The end is wide open,' he said.

'What does that mean?' she said.

'I think he was putting it in her hands.'

Then the kitchen ceiling started leaking and they forgot all about it.

★

She was as surprised as anyone when the lawyer read her mother's will. The family had two properties. The house in Devonport and the farm were both left to her and her brothers equally, but she got to decide what happened to the farm. Apparently, that was what her mother had wanted. She spoke with the lawyer right after, making her brothers wait outside. The lawyer told her what she already knew: she couldn't afford rates and maintenance on two properties. He said keep the house, sell the farm.

'Forget about Kumeu,' he said. 'That's my advice.'

So she made the call. For the last six weeks the farm has been on the market, and dozens of people have made offers and asked to bring the auction forward, but she has remained firm, told them she was going to wait.

Last night, her brothers tried one last time to talk her out of selling. They wanted to convert the farm into a retreat for the end days. They wanted to build pods on the land, grow crops, harness the stream for drinking water, kill cattle for food. They had never killed anything in their whole lives. They didn't know that when she got sick of their dreams—when she said, 'Enough already, the decision's made'—and walked out the front door, she didn't walk down into town but slipped around the back to Pat's flat. She passed right by the room where they sat bitching.

Later, after a few more drinks, they tried calling her, texting her: 'we need more time … If you could see the plans … if you could just understand …'

If only they'd known they could have walked across the back yard, knocked on the door. Their little sister was twenty metres away, wrapped around the teacher, desperately, desperately trying to get out of her head.

★

It is one of the most memorable moments of her life. She is twelve years old. A Sunday afternoon at the farm, sitting under the oak at the end of the long table. Her brothers are playing in the fields. She is alone with the adults. It could be the day of the photo.

She is chewing a crust, listening, when she sees it in the distance. Trees shaking. Birds taking off. She tries to speak but everyone ignores her. Speaks over her. Trees closer whip back and forth; the wind takes shape, changes direction, carves through fields. It is so easy to see it frightens her. She grabs the table and braces. Then it doesn't really matter—the wind hits; everyone's screaming and swearing, plates and glasses are flying, and everything is immense, overwhelming. But not like she expected. Of all the things she feels it is relief she remembers most—because for the first time she witnessed something no one else had. She saw it coming.

★

'How are the girls?' she says, watching the breeze play with his hair.
 'The girls?'
 'Your girls.'
 He looks surprised. 'You never ask about them.'
 'Would you be sad to leave them? Do you miss them?'
 'Of course I do.'
 She nods. 'How come it didn't work out between you two?'
 'How come you never learned to drive?'
 'You first,' she says.
 He says, 'It wasn't what either of us wanted. It never was.'

★

She wants to tell him, she really does. All afternoon she has opportunities. Like while they are sitting by the road waiting for coffee and he finally asks her, 'So, how much?'
 'How much?' she asks, keeping her face blank.
 'Did you get what you wanted?'
 'It's about what we thought.'
 'That's good.' He drinks his coffee in gulps. 'Not yet twenty-five and you're rich.'
 'You live in my back yard,' she says, laughing to keep it light. 'This can't come as a surprise.'

But afterwards she thinks of his life before her and wonders just how different, how much harder, it must have been.

She gets another chance in the supermarket as they look for something to eat. He says, 'What will you do with it?'

'With the money?'

'Yes, with the money.'

'Any bright ideas?' she says.

'None,' he says.

And again, one last time, as they go through self-checkout. He says, 'Who gets Devonport?'

'Don't worry,' she wanted to say. 'You can stay. No matter what happens, you can stay.'

★

Eventually, after they eat an early dinner at his little table and are back lying on the bed, he tells her.

'I saw an email from Ryanair a while back. I guessed Rome.'

'They saw smoke in Rome,' she says, her eyes wide like she can't believe it.

'I gave you an opening.'

'You were close,' she says. 'But no, Hong Kong. At least to begin.'

'I'll take you to the airport.'

'Good.' She tries to smile. 'So, now's your chance. Tell me everything you hate about me.'

'There's nothing,' he says and rubs his face.

She wants to hug him now but instead she lies still beside him. She already knows she won't see him again no matter what else they say. And though she tries to ignore it a part of her is wondering: why doesn't he do something? Why doesn't he reach over and shake me as hard as he can?

Except she already knows why.

He thinks she has to go. She hasn't ever really had a life and now she can afford one. Deep down he knows she's leaving for no good reason. Both of them know it. But Annie's head hurts and her eyes are burning and she can't stop now. She's too far gone already.

★

'You never asked me anything,' he says. 'That was the only red flag.'

They are trapped in traffic on the southern motorway. They should have taken their time but once it was out they had to move.

She thinks, this is not how it's meant to go.

'That's not true.'

'Why do I teach?'

'I don't know.'

'Exactly.'

He's right. She has never cared about knowing him. All she wants to ask him now is what happened to the kid with the love letter. But she decides to leave it. The rest will be silence.

Then he surprises her.

He says, 'You just don't get it. You don't even realise this doesn't happen, that what we have … Listen, I want you to remember this. See that guy yelling at his kids? I want you to remember that fucking guy yelling at his kids. All I want …' he says, but he never tells her what he wants. He stops and breathes. He closes his eyes.

She thinks, and *now* he's done.

And she's right. They're pulling into the drop-off zone and he's killing the ignition and he's getting her bags and he doesn't say a word the entire time. She's not speaking either. She's looking at him stacking the trolley and she's suddenly unsure about everything. The ground isn't stable and the sky's gone dark; there's a ringing in her ears and she's wondering about all the important stuff. She's thinking, but who will wait on yellow lines for me, and who will bring a blanket to the park, and who, who will carry my coffee down to the sea?

NICHOLAS WRIGHT

Yoke

You will do well to have the roots
by the hand. A severable plant
resilient, or so it's said
the word being used so often.
And here's a thirsty newcomer, well fed
perfectly formed—*adventitious*.
Sprung traces of the grand design
recur in the stolon followers—more
than modest hands might manage, hands
that could be busy with other work.

Lunch, and all the talk of feeding heads.
At the bottom of the garden
an enormous civic body, thighs
white-clad in rubber, ploughs
holy as a farmer, the stream
that runs like an idea beneath
the flight path. Yet another laureate
is talking about the human condition.
Down there the council addles goose eggs
the slick root of an eel following.

VAUGHAN RAPATAHANA

painting

in papatoetoe
I painted the picket fence,
proverbial white it was,
one cliché
bordering another:
the quarter-acre section.

at pakaraka
the house was ancient mariner,
forever demanding attention.
spraying stain across its porticos,
while white it was,
did little to muzzle its carious sneer.

kei te ūrupa o tutua
I brushstroked the stumbling boundary.
white it was,
an attempt to contain
the hermaphroditic grass
sprouting here   and   over   there.

in santo tomas
I daubed the agonal stone wall.
white it was,
highlighting the guava/papaya climbers
clambering across the top
like *serpiginous snakes*.

inside tin yan complex
I coated every possible panel.
white it was,
vivifying for a while
the drab, scratched surfaces
that were old men dying.

I am still painting.
white it is,
some sort of scrupulosity
to shroud the chthonic shades
squatting everywhere underneath
               like sialoquent dogs.

I'll do this until I die.

NICOLA ANDREWS

Self-driving Cars

You would have been so interested to hear about them—
sensors and cameras fanning out like a winning hand,
the weeks of peering warily from behind blackout curtains
as they made sporadic u-turns in my unassuming cul-de-sac,
the night bursting open to an outbreak of malfunction,
crumpled metal slung around a power pole, lights flashing

You would have been so curious, phone pressed to ear—
asking how it feels to spot a whirring phantom on the street,
the sharp inhale of double-take braving the zebra crossing,
eerier still, a lone passenger, slouching and chauffeurless,
a vine of zeroes and ones wreathing around the windows,
silhouettes framed and rushing towards their futurity.

You would have really howled to hear the headlines—
algorithmic automatons in orange dunce caps smacking
into fire trucks, undone by uncured cement, so upset
by rising steam. Like listless teenagers, crippled without
cellphone service. A road-cone coronation, upturned
like a too-quick ruling. Swerving, then stalled. Like favour.

Sometimes I cannot overthrow my disquiet, and wonder:
Would a self-driving car have braked in time? Would their
cameras have detected the bones in your small frame,
protected your lungs from puncturing like blown-out airbags?
I'm not sure, and there are some things we are not meant
to know. But I'm sorry you never arrived here, to the future.

EMMA NEALE

Mistranslation

As a child when she could be sure
her mother wouldn't ride the anger horse
she liked to play little elegant afternoons.
The sun took her in tiny stinging bites
as she sat quietly with her thin plastic dolls,
role models of pink glow and hollow serene
while a mirror noticed her father's slippers
fill with shadows.
Yes, he was always
a very *perhaps* man
at work late even on Sundays
wearing his handsome talent out.

GREG JUDKINS

The Children

As if it is left to the dark
rain-glossed trees burdened
with bright ripe citrus
and the long-fingered kikuyu that prowls
the weathered board house
to do something
about the children.

KATE VAN DER DRIFT

Earth Matters

1 Apples (after Gabrielle)
2 Esk Valley Orchard (after Gabrielle)
3 Apples II (after Gabrielle)
4 Holden (after Gabrielle)
5 SH 5 (after Gabrielle)
6 Apples III (after Gabrielle)
7 Esk River Mouth (after Gabrielle)
8 Roses (after Gabrielle)

All works archival pigment prints, 750 x 1000mm, 2023

In Kate van der Drift's *Earth Matters*, we observe Papatūānuku in a state of grief and the slow recalibration that occurs in the wake of this grief. We are witness to the tension between the redistribution of silt/whenua as severe erosion, combined with detrimental human-induced (toxic) elements. For many, this silt is a waste material that impedes the day-to-day functioning and productivity of the land—for others, the soil and silt is whenua, a treasured resource and taonga. Through van der Drift's sensitive contemplation, our gaze falls on the shrouding of the land by sediment; there is a quietness as her lens listens in for the mauri or life essence of Papatūānuku that vibrates beneath and throughout this newly dispersed overlay. Van der Drift urges us to look upon this earthly matter in the aftermath of Cyclone Gabrielle and to witness the complexity and delicacy of the earth's tender healing.

— Lynley Edmeades

JAMES O'SULLIVAN

A Bit of a Mess

Late one night while Mum is at a friend's getting pissed, I'm in my bedroom trying to read *Wuthering Heights*, which is a boring-as book Mrs Coxon set us to read for English, when I hear this grunting and gasping coming from my sister's room next door, the walls being paper thin and the wallpaper peeling and the plaster crumbling beneath that. Maybe she thinks I'm asleep at this hour but she's not holding back. I can only put up with this disgusting noise for so long, so I storm out of my room and I'm about to bang on her door and tell the guy she's got in there to clear off, thinking it's some loser who's sneaked in through her window, when who should come out but Mum's boyfriend Brody. I tell him he's a pervert and she's not even sixteen, and he says she's fifteen and near enough, and furthermore, he says I'm getting the bashing of my life if I report this to Mum. Well, as you can imagine, the first thing I do when Mum gets home, looking pretty smashed I may add, is tell her what her deadbeat boyfriend's been up to. I'm expecting to be thanked for this service but the boozed-up old cow clips me on the head and tells me not to tell such filthy lies. She says she knows I don't get along with her new man but there's no cause to be telling such damaging untruths. I tell her I heard them myself going at it hammer and thongs and she can ask my sister. Brody looms over me and says it's either I move out or he teaches me not to say such lies. Mum doesn't even back me up. Instead she leans against the wall for support because she's too pissed to stand up straight, and she says that me moving out would be for the best considering I don't get along with her new man. Which is fine by me because I don't like this house much anyway, especially the hole in the floor in the corridor that the landlord is never going to fix. Sometimes you can see a rat poking its little pointy head up through it. I tell Mum I knew from the start I wasn't contemptible with Brody. Mum tells me the word I'm looking for is compatible. Whatever, the upshoot is, I'm packed off to my Uncle Ben's, who lives out of town in a shitty little rundown house in the middle of a cow paddock. The thing about Uncle Ben is that he's bat crazy. He flies American flags on his front lawn and he also has Vote for Trump signs stuck on his house, and funny ideas about the world. The first thing he asks me when I turn up with my suitcase and my *Wuthering Heights* book is if I have been immunised, because he doesn't permit immunised people in his house, kind of like an anti-vaccine pass thing. Well, I tell the crazy bastard I didn't have much choice as people kept sticking needles into my arm because I wouldn't be able to go to places if I didn't let them. He tells me I've been abused by the system and he'll teach me some things so I can be free of oppression and mind control. After giving me special dispensing to enter his house, he sets me up in this small-as room at the back that's really just a sunporch. And I know straight away the house is not fit for human hibernation because it smells of old socks, the dishes are piled up on the benches, the mice feed on the leftovers stuck to the plates, and there's some sort of plant growing in the shower. Not to mention the rats I can hear scurrying around in the ceiling. But it's not just me at Uncle Ben's: he has a mate called Titus, an old Māori guy who's all in for self-determination, and he's stuck up that white and red and black flag they got, next to the American flag, and he says Trump is the only man that can solve the ills of the world. I'm somewhat septical about his theories myself but I keep my head down and try to read this bloody book, which is still boring as, so I give up and watch the movie of the book, which is a brilliant scheme I think, until I blow it by telling Mrs Coxon in class that Heathcliff (the boss bad guy in the book) is Black, to which she says, he is not Black, to which I reply, of course he's Black, to which she says, no, he is not, and I can't stop my stupid mouth from blurting out, well, he's Black in the movie I saw, which pretty much causes the cat to jump out of the bag, so she tells me to keep reading the book and no cheating this time. And this humiliates me in front of the class, who have a good laugh at my object stupidity, so when I get back from school to Uncle Ben's I'm in a bad-as mood, and I tell him the windows are breezy in the old sunporch and it gets cold at night and what the hell is that thing growing in the shower? And does he know he's got rodents ingesting his house? He tells me I'll just have to put up with it, the rats don't hurt anyone, and where do I think I am living anyway, in a palace? He further says that if the guvment wasn't robbing everybody blind we'd all be living like lords. Titus, who is always hanging around, says this is how Māori have always had to live because of the colonial oppressors, and I tell him it's not even his bloody house so why is he complaining? Uncle Ben puts in that any oppressed Māori is welcome in his house, and one day Trump will free all the oppressed peoples, and the Q army will rise up and put Jacinda Ardern in jail for crimes against humanity. I make the mistake of saying I think Cindy is pretty hot, to which Uncle Ben says he'd rather get his end away in a light socket. So this is about the intellectual level of our conversations, that is, whether or not we fancy an ex-prime minister, and considering the only other topics of conversation are if I want to join the Q army, or if the Covid vaccine is a mind-control drug, I decide to go to my room, which is really a draughty old sunporch, and read *Wuthering Heights* and stare up at the mould on the ceiling and try to make pictures of it like it was clouds. The book doesn't get much better and the boss bad guy is plotting revenges and beating up on women and hating everybody and I think I get enough of that in the real world, so I don't need to read it in a book. And listening to the rats in the ceiling I start thinking home could be the better option. It doesn't take long for things to come to a head at Uncle Ben's anyway, pretty much when Uncle Ben and Titus get proper pissed one night on homemade feijoa wine that tastes like feijoa cordial. They start marching around the house with guns saying the guvment is going to have to take them out of their cold dead hands. And that's about it for me, so I pack up my shit in my suitcase along with bloody *Wuthering Heights* and call Mum and say she's got to take me back because insane people are running around here with guns, and if she doesn't take me back I'm going to have the filth over to arrest the lot of them. She reluctantly comes over and tells Uncle Ben perhaps he should put the guns away, and Uncle Ben tells her to mind her own bloody business and if she wants to be a brainwashed sheep licking Cindy's feet then that's her problem, but she shouldn't expect him to be so stupid. Mum tells him he's an idiot and the guvment isn't interested in those old farmer's guns that probably don't work anyway. Thankfully, Uncle Ben and Titus eventually put down the old firearms and take out their frustrations on woke people on Twitter, and while they're crowding around the computer shouting, Mum tells me to jump in the car and we head home. And if you think my life gets much better from here on in, well, guess again, because the second I get home my sister and Mum's boyfriend Brody are having this massive-as shouting match in the corridor, and my sister is saying she's sick of all the secrecy and she wants to run off with Brody and have a family, and Mum shouts at her not to tell such terrible lies and she further adds that now will be a good time to tell my sister and me and everyone else that she is pregnant and we will soon have another brother or sister. This is meant to suck the wind out of our sails, but not my sister, who shoots straight back at Mum that she is also pregnant and Mum should expect a grandson or a granddaughter. Brody is standing there looking pretty sick and suddenly Mum realises the truth of the matter. She puts her head in her hands and starts sobbing, which I don't like to see. She may be a grumpy old cow with a pennant for deadbeat losers, but she's still my mum. Brody quietly asks my sister if the baby is his. And my sister says yes, of course it is, or if it's not his then it could be Jarvis's from school, or maybe the school maintenance guy's, or possibly Michael who's in a roadworks gang, or Taine the farmhand, or Greg who does nothing in particular, or perhaps it could be Dave's, but she hopes not because she thinks they're distantly related and the baby could come out a mutant with no chin. And Mum looks up and says, but cousin Dave is just a boy, and my sister says he wasn't when she was last with him. Mum goes back to sobbing, while Brody starts ranting and raving that he'll bash every guy my sister's been with, and my sister says if Brody doesn't throw his lot in with her she'll go to the pigs and tell them she's only fifteen and she'll lay a complaint. To which Brody responds that a complaint seems to be about the only thing she hasn't laid. My sister resents the application that she is free and loose and heads for the front door and says she'll go to the coppers right now and say she's been abused. Brody goes after her but puts his foot through the hole in the floor, crumples in a heap and screams in pain, which causes my sister to hurry back to him saying she's sorry and they will always be together. Mum just crouches on the floor and cries and says there's no justice in this world anymore, and men were just designed to make her life miserable. It's all a bit of a mess really, so I go to my room and start reading *Wuthering Heights* again. The boss bad guy is bashing his head against a tree because he doesn't like how the world is, which is kind of like what I feel like doing, so the book's starting to make a bit more sense now.

NICOLA THORSTENSEN

Papering

Clydesdales take the strain
in one half of the room,
haul black Cobb & Co coaches
across the wallpaper's textured terrain.

This side of the divide,
two walls are repapered,
a coffee stain design,
no sharp lines, an easy match.

Months back, the room buzzed with industry.
We kids applied size to the walls
using broad brushes
while Mum and Dad pulled paper
through the paste trough
mounted on an old door.

Plumbline steadied,
they worked each length into place,
coaxed out air bubbles,
trimmed slivers of waste
with the orange Stanley knife.

Now Mum wants to hire a paperhanger
to finish the task.
Without Dad, she says she can't face
the last wall's blank plaster.

But some skills slow-seep.
Copying Dad's cadence,
I sang before I could speak,
standing on the pew,
hymn book upside down.

Mum and I make a good job of it,
this papering over,
this carry-on.

CHRIS CANTILLON

First Charge

High sky a nightlong howl (a sleeper awake)
dive winds chased across the gable tip
cables joins wrenched ripped, boards loosed and flapped
the farmhouse holding on, is cold here
and lonely my husband away (again)
a blame between us, he or me who
couldn't have children, the woman bears it
year ago I listed us as fosters
psych-tested okayed, our first charge arrives tomorrow (today) what will I be like

MICHELLE DUFF

Sweetie

Bro, hard. You seen Dave much lately? Nah, he's on the down-low eh—you hear what happened? Maaaate. You're gonna love this. Strap in, son.

So he meets this chick in The Railway, right, buys her a drink, you know they've got two for one bourbons on a Friday or whatever? Yeah, last weekend. So they're smashing those back, they're dancing haaardout, she's all over him, man, shaking her arse and shit. Wearing some of those little shiny short things they all wear.

And then Dave like sees his chance, he's all let's go for a walk, and they leave the club and they're walking across that grassy bit just outside Booties? You know it? Yeah yeah, where Stevo pulled those rarkies after prizegiving, kinda opposite that weird park thing where the carnies put up their tents.

Na, bro. I'm good, you have it.

So yeah, they're walking along and he's like sweet, man, I'm nailing this. He's got her up against a tree and that, feeling her up, she's got these real big titties. Yeah, like in between Brandy and Steph, maybe? Na, bigger than that.

Me? Na, arse all the way. Any more than a handful's a waste, eh. Haha.

Yeah, anyway he's faaarking hooning away on those, like got his face in there and everything, flapping away like a baby duck, fucking motorboating, man. Quacking and shit. I know, bro! Like, fully. In there. So then he sees this bush and he's like that's a bit of me, get her in there, seal the deal, you know.

But then she's all like swaying, and all 'I can't' and 'I feel sick', so he sees that's not gonna work, so then he tries to get her to give him a blowie but she's unkeen, so then he kisses her again to sweeten her up, right, and he's like, 'Can we go back to yours?' Seductive as.

You've seen him do it, eh? Blue-as eyes. Chicks love him. Yeah, I asked him once eh, and he was like, 'Bro, just nod heaps when they're talking, it makes them think you're listening, and then tell them how much you love your mum. They think it's cute.'

Anyway they can't go back to hers—she lives out of town. Dave's got a room at his parents' hotel for the night, it's like a five-minute walk. Yeah man, they own it. Stays there cos it's easier to take chicks back there on the weekend. Fucking sweet, right? But that night his parents are staying there too for some event or some shit, and he's thinking he doesn't want to take her back there because of the old lady, you know, he's like son of the year or whatever, they think the sun shines out his arse. Yeah, bro. He's at med school. But then he's like fuck it, may as well, she's fucking hot, he can just call her a cab or give her some money or whatever after, and he's been like *hanging out* ever since he and Brandy broke up, right?

Ehh? How did you not know? Bro, eeeeeeeveryone knows. He came home to find her fucking his flatmate. For real. Like, for *real* for real. Yeah na, you won't believe this, it's faarking priceless.

It was Andy's twenty-first—yeah, that's the flatmate—and Brandy was being a skank, just rubbing all over Andy like a sponge or some shit, like she was putting him through a carwash, swish-swish-swish, you know, yeah, *yeah* bro! Hahahaha. You'd give her one, eh. Yeah, for sure, bro. I'd be in there, you know it. She's tight as.

Na, I was outside. Eric saw the whole thing.

I used to go to primary school with her, eh. She was all right back then. Dunno what went wrong.

Yeah so she's dancing all over Andy and he's whispering in her ear or whatever and the bro Dave has her up about it, right there on the d-floor, like why you got to be such a slut, you're a fucking embarrassment. Then Shanté reckons she saw Dave bailing Brandy up against the fence, like hardout up in her face, yeah. Just screaming at her. I dunno, this far? Yeah, dunno. He might've. Haaard agree, bro. Can't let 'em get away with that shit. You've seen the way she walks around too, eh, like she's miss fucking universe.

Anyway it turns out Dave was right not to let her off the hook because later on he's like where the fuck is she? And then we all pile in the car back to his and when we get back we can't find the bong like anywhere—yeah, the bucky, that's the one, eh, it's way better. Yup, waaasted—yeah man, we tried the apple too, tastes nice, eh? Just chuck the ol' hole in the back, it's real fruity, eh. Fruity as. No homo.

So the door to Andy's room is closed and Dave is knocking on it. There's no answer but we're hanging out for a sesh, eh, and no one's got any papers so he puts his ear against the door and he can hear someone moaning and starts thinking what the fuck, is everything okay? He starts worrying, he's thinking, man, Andy did that yardy earlier, like he might need some help, maybe he's choking on his own vomit or whatever, so he pushes the door open and then—then, bro—he sees a chick on top of Andy like fully naked, and for a second he's like 'yeeeaaah boi', and then she like kind of looks and screams or whatever and it's Brandy.

Oi, chuck us a twennie for gas? Sweet. Wanna get a slab on the way? Na, that stuff's horrible. Cody's all the way. Eight-per-centers. What the fuck? Court case in a can. *You're* a court case in a can, bro, haha. They gotta catch me first.

Na, he just left the room. Said he didn't care about her anyway. And get this, Andy comes out in the morning and we all like give him a standing ovation, and Dave goes to shake his hand, like well played, bro, well fucking played. You beat me to it that time, haha. Took her down with the ol' Brandy-Andy one-two combo. Branandy. Andy doesn't really look Dave in the eye or put his hand out and it's a bit weird, like c'mon Andy, mate, it's funny, right? Take a joke.

Na, dunno, she probably just crawled out like a fucking cockroach, eh, stomp on her as she goes past. Squish her into the carpet, eh bro.

Yeah, true? Na, I didn't hear that. Shit. Well, yeah, that's kinda sad, eh, but she always was a bit of a psycho. Just like her mum, eh, runs in that family—have you seen their house? Bro. I went there heaps when we were kids. Paru as, just like one couch and a rickety-as table. And when I say rickety, I mean ric–ke–ty, like you could have splintered it up into kindling in about half a second. Yeah, we were pretty good mates in primary school, eh. Her mum was pretty nice actually. Used to make us sandwiches and tuck us into bed and everything. Na, haha. Nothing like that. But yeah, she was chill then. She had this cute little playhouse. We used to hang out in there and she used to make us come up with all these stories, like acting out fairytales … um. Yeah. Weird, right? Stupid kids.

Yeah, so, fuck knows.

Oi, but I tell you what did happen—like a week later she comes back to the flat and all the boys are there, it was the night the final was on. Yeah, bro. Wallabies. So we're all sitting around and Brandy comes screeching in like a fucking harpie, rips the curtains back and she's just standing there right in front of the TV. Steph's there too, looking sour as. And she's got all these—what do you call 'em—momentoes or whatever, and she walks up to Dave and tips the box over his head and this giant dragon he reckons he gave her for Christmas once that cost heaps from Lotz of Potz like *nails* him right on the dome, and his head is pissing blood, and she's yelling, 'Here you go, you cheating cunt, you're an abuser, like fuck you, here's all your shit, now give me back Sweetie.'

Oh. Yeah, Dave cheated on her loads, bro. Pass that lighter?

Sweetie's their rabbit. They like bought it together. Brandy reckons she paid for it and always looked after it so it should be hers. But honestly, bro, Dave loved that rabbit. We all did. He used to take her out and stroke her for hours, sing her little lullabies. She was cute as, real furry, she'd snuggle up to you if you went to pick her up. She loved carrots, she'd like nibble them out of your hand and it was tickly as on your skin, and she'd run around the house at night with her little tail bobbing up and down. But, yeah, Dave wouldn't have put it past Brandy to pull some crafty shit so he had already taken Sweetie around to the hotel. They've got some grass out the back, so he made a little hutch for her to run around in, and he was getting the hotel staff to bring her inside in her cage at night. Safe as. So when Brandy asks for Sweetie he just sits back all smug and he's like, 'I got rid of her.' Brandy stares at him and she doesn't say anything—like bro, you coulda heard a pin drop—and then she just walks out.

We're all sat there like *whaaaaat?*

Still, you have to hand it to Brandy. That was a pretty ballsy move, eh, to bust in like that and let him have it. You should have seen his face, man. He was catching flies.

What's that? Oh, yeah. The other chick.

So after Brandy fucks him over Dave goes through a real dry spell and all the girls are trying to tell him it's his fault, you know, acting like he was the one being a dick to her when he's just trying to keep her in line. Yeah, they call it gaslighting, bro—trying to make her think she's crazy. Yeah, I know, bullshit. As if he needs to try.

Anyway this girl starts hitting on him in the pub. They're in the park, they're walking back to his, and then she turns to him and she's like, 'Dave, that's your name, eh? What's your last name?' and he's like, 'Lampie', and she's like, 'Cool, just checking', and he's thinking okaaay, why do you even need to know that, you know? But she's like oh, 'I think you might know my cousin', but also he doesn't really care, he just wants to fucking demo her so bad.

So they get back to his hotel room and she pulls out a bottle of tequila and they're slamming back all these shots, then they get naked. He reckons she's fit as, like a solid 8. Maybe a 9. Then he starts giving her head and she's loving it. She keeps on yelling 'Now! Now!' like at the top of her lungs—he has to keep telling her to be quiet. Yeah, bro. But oi, he doesn't even get to fuck her. He's so toasted he just falls asleep mid-pussy.

When he wakes up it's daytime and he's got the dries and the first thing he thinks is damn, hope that chick's not still here, and when he rolls over he's on his own. So he's like, thank god. Dodged a bullet. He rolls back over to go to sleep but there's all this sand in his bed and it smells kinda weird in his room and then his mum's banging on the door, like, 'Davey! Get out here now!' He's thinking, Jesus, hold your fucking horses, woman, then he goes to get up and when he pulls back the covers, bro, it ain't sand, there's *rabbit poo* everywhere, like all through his bed, between his legs, those little yellow pellets are even stuck to his *ball sacks*, bro! I don't even know where someone would get that much rabbit shit.

He gets out of bed and squashes it into the carpet. He's like dry-retching, and the first thing he thinks is where's Sweetie? Her cage isn't in the corner of his room. He thinks maybe he moved it so he's looking around, then he thinks he might have left it out at the hutch, so he goes outside and his olds are just standing there with their arms crossed like 'What is the meaning of this, young man?' and he looks and he's like faaaark. On the outside of his room someone's spray-painted the word S E X P E S T.

Dave got a bad feeling. He's calling all over, like 'Sweetie! *Sweeeetie!*' and he goes out to the hutch and there's like five rabbits stuffed inside all staring at him with their beady eyes but none of them are Sweetie. She's gone. Just like vanished into thin air. Poof. No homo.

Dunno, man. Buzzy as. Didn't see anything. Na, he didn't get her name.

Brandy? Yeah, she moved in with Andy. He's totally pussy-whipped. Didn't even say hi when I saw him in town. What a stink cunt.

DAVID EGGLETON

The Plastisphere

Ocean's on a bender, it's a hot tub ocean,
gulping chemicals, scavenging microplastics,
chest deep in sea-wasps, pink sacs of box-jellies.
How drastic is plastic now? Confetti afloat,
it's fallen like coloured rain made from nurdles,
bait nets, gill nets, shrimp nets, trawl nets,
polyurethane and nylon bits that swim for it.

Each coast washes up plastic souvenirs
that may, while broken, last a hundred years.
A single-use plastic planet's cling-wrapped;
forever residues in the deep marine crumble,
with nowhere to flush away those flakes
that circulate in trillions, vaster than empires;
the unfurling surf laden with apocalypse.

Crab Nebula glows with the fiery filaments
of a supernova from a millennium ago.
Ammonite heads are buried deep in sand.
Gas fields flare on the Taranaki coast:
Kapuni, Māui, Pohukura, Kupe.
Vistas of cities on web-cams glow like jewels.
We stare at stars that represent ancestors ablaze.

KRISTIN KELLY

Underneath it All

As an eight-year-old I used to retreat to my bedroom with a collection of snacks and pretend I was marooned on an island and they were my only sustenance until I either built a raft or was pecked to death by seagulls. The snacks comprised a mix of things I could get past my parents—some sliced fruit usually, and maybe a few pieces of liquorice which I would chew slowly, purposefully, like a goat with its cud. The pièces de résistance of my rations were the shot glasses full of milk and Ribena that I would place carefully on my wooden floor and drink, sip by tiny sip.

Did you know that you can survive up to three months without food, but only three days without water? I did. I would arch my neck backwards into a geometric equation so that I could drain every last drop, staining my teeth purple and growing on my upper lip a moustache of blue-top.

While after a few years I stopped playing this game, I maintained the conviction that these were the two options: save yourself or perish. In the interim: moderate your juice intake. After my dad's aneurysm I began to apply this way of thinking to money. 'The Brain Injury Fund', I called my savings account, where I socked away the bulk of the meagre wages I made selling hotdogs and dancing in a tiger suit. It seemed inevitable to me in my teenage years that another great tragedy would befall us and at least with $12.75 per hour I could—while not prevent it—reduce some of the collateral damage.

I was constantly doing sums in my head. These were not just about the $3.50 muesli slice that was before me, but also about how the year before I had bought a sweatshirt with umbrellas on it for $5 from the Vinnies and that if I hadn't got that sweatshirt, in two years' time I could have justified the giant light-up picture of Jesus I coveted with an irony equal in measure to my desperation.

I judged people, too, when they purchased things I considered frivolous, which was everything. *I mean Converses*, I would think, when a classmate debuted a new pair of high-tops. *Not for me, thanks. I'll go barefoot.*

Even when I was salaried and began making what my parents referred to as 'Real Money', I continued to scrounge like I was on the verge of insolvency. 'Seven dollars!' I would say, waving in front of my friends a sweat-stained op-shop dress two sizes too big. 'Can you believe it?' They always could.

My behaviour drove everyone I knew crazy, but Esther, who got updates on my purchases in a stream of consciousness that bordered on Kerouac, found it particularly frustrating. One day, when I was talking about getting through my undergrad degree without a student loan, she retorted, 'Well, I got through mine with my mental health intact.'

'She's quite good at that, isn't she, those truth bombs?' my psychiatrist remarked years later when I recounted this story, my mental health still poor, Esther's student loan at $65k. 'Yes,' I said. 'Yes, she is.'

Esther was also delighted when I messaged her one Saturday morning agreeing to go shopping at Bendon. After staying at my apartment the night before she had got up early to go to her nephew's soccer game, leaving the offer of a shopping trip on the table. 'Let's do it,' I told her, sitting on my couch, mug of filter coffee in hand. 'Yes!' she replied. Then she sent me a video of five-year-olds, all of them hovering around the ball as if drawn to it by a powerful magnetic force. *Spread out, you idiots*, I thought, swirling my dregs. *This game is a team sport.*

⋆

Esther was determined that I buy a matching set of lingerie. 'Sexy!' she said.

'Only if they're on sale, okay?' I told her as we browsed.

She pointed at a corset, red and silky with decorative buttons down the front. 'What about this?' She whirled to face me, swiping it off the rack so it dangled in front of my face, a cherry begging to be popped.

'Absolutely not,' I said, migrating towards a bra the same colour as my skin, which resembled, upon closer inspection, a pair of saggy testicles.

'Not flesh-coloured,' she said. 'Maybe something black. Something you want to rip off.'

This was how she convinced me I should get undies as well as a bra. 'You know I only like cotton,' I whined. 'Synthetics give me thrush.'

'Yes,' she replied, 'but the point is you won't be wearing them for long. You'll have them on, and then ten seconds later you'll be naked.'

As much as this was an exercise in spending money, it was also an exercise in reconnecting with my sexuality. 'I get it now!' I had messaged Esther about a month before. 'I get why women have to wear panty liners!' I had recently come off the antidepressant I had been on for the past two years—one that made sex about as interesting to me as watching the infomercial channel. Compression socks. Doggy style. It was all the same.

'But now even animals can tell I'm on heat!' I continued. I had walked by him one morning, a beast of a mutt with a head the size and weight of a four-month-old baby. While I chatted to his mum, a kindly woman who ended every conversation with 'God bless you. Have a good day,' things I wasn't sure I believed in, he placed his paws on my right thigh. Then, as he mounted my leg, he looked up at me imploringly with big, sad brown eyes.

'No,' I said to him gently. 'No, we're not going to do that.'

'But he was still a good boy,' I told my friend Amy later when detailing our encounter. 'Very, very polite.'

★

I picked up a shiny green bra, slightly mermaidesque and fifty percent off. 'What about this?' I asked Esther, who was standing to my left, peering over my shoulder.

She shook her head disapprovingly. 'My mother just bought that one.'

I put it back on the rack.

We wandered about the shop doing this for around half an hour. I would identify something and Esther would veto it, usually on the basis of its appearance, and then she would identify something else and I would veto it, usually on the basis of its price. 'Just try them, Kristin,' she said eventually, marching me to the changing rooms. 'Just try.'

They're glorious, Bendon's changing rooms. Senselessly appropriative but beautifully appointed with shoji doors and murals of happy birds nesting in sakuras. 'Do you think they'd noticed if I walked out in that?' I asked Esther as I took off my sweatshirt, nodding at the full-length kimono that hung on the wall for decoration.

'Yes,' she replied, hooking up the clasps of the bra I'd just put on.

It was black, sheer, conceptually hot. 'But look!' I demanded, standing before the mirror. 'Look what it's done to the shape of my breasts!' They had been raised, flattened and shifted apart from each other as though each was trying to escape into the corresponding armpit. *Like little blob fish*, I thought, cupping them with my hands.

The next set was a disaster too, the undies sitting directly beneath the fleshiest part of my stomach so that I looked like a giant diapered toddler. I groaned. 'Yeah, that's really bad,' Esther said, leaving to gather some different sizes and styles.

She did this twice while I stood alone in the changing room looking at myself in the full-length mirror, critiquing every visible inch of my skin. Saggy butt, dimpled thighs, doughy stomach, masculine shoulders and a jawline so asymmetrical it looked like it had been designed by the architect of Sydney's Opera House. *I might have a sex drive, but who*, I wondered, *would want to have sex with me?*

★

Esther slid the door open without knocking.

'Warning!' I shouted. 'I need some warning!' She had been quick that time, but the next time she took a lot longer and as I waited, I began to panic. What if she had left? What if she had decided she was as sick of me as I was myself?

'And then I thought, would I just keep sitting here?' I gasped at her when she returned, 'sitting by myself in my flesh-coloured underwear and waiting?' She laughed, remarking that even if that did happen, I had everything I needed: my clothes, my bag, my phone. She was right, obviously, but none of that mattered. The point was I would have been abandoned. All alone, without any liquid, stranded in a cubicle modelled on an island.

The set that Esther brought back, the one I eventually bought, was black, made of lace but not the dainty kind. It was the statement dominatrix kind— all fishnet and thick black stripes. *This*, I thought as I paid for it, *is the kind of thing that people who other people want to have sex with wear.*

'I wasn't sure you would actually get anything,' Esther said as we walked back towards her car. 'Yeah, neither was I,' I replied, my purchase tucked safely into my small leather backpack. I had bought it for $25 from a second-hand shop so it was fine on balance, I reasoned, to fill it with $90 worth of nylon. 'Well, I'm really glad you did,' she continued, 'because I did not get through your depression last year for you to *not* buy that set.'

It was a fair call. When the guy I had been in a situationship with broke up with me, or rather, failed to break up with his girlfriend, Esther had flown back to Wellington early from her parents' place in Blenheim and turned up at my apartment.

'What are you doing here?' I had sobbed.

I whipped out this line in various forms over the following year as she consistently showed up for me, always for reasons completely beyond my comprehension. 'Kristin,' she said one evening, a ginger beer in hand, 'I will always be here on your couch with you eating Thai food. The only thing that is going to change in this relationship is your level of depression.'

Secure in the friendship, a few months after we went underwear shopping I messaged her while standing in my room, surveying all that I had just dumped on my bed.

'I just wanted to leave you a voice message so that you would give me praise,' I said, and proceeded to detail how earlier that day I had gone to the Bendon Outlet Store in Tawa and spent $120 on two bras and six pairs of undies. 'You know, I put on an old pair this morning,' I told her, 'that was so pathetic, I was like, *I can't do this anymore*.' The situation had been, as I explained, dire. The elastic around the waist was shot so the undies slid down my butt, while at the front my pubic hair poked through the thinning fabric, tiny tentacles, all of them reaching out towards a more dignified existence.

Esther's reply was instantaneous. She began and ended her voice message by telling me how proud of me she was. Then, in between, she listed the three key reasons. I had not gone, as I usually did, to Kmart where I bought things in six-packs. I had gone by myself. I was buying stuff I needed because I needed it and, she told me, because I deserved it. 'With your sexy arse,' she said—a photo of which she had captured from our earlier shopping excursion—'you need some cute, non-holey undies.'

★

I didn't hear her message until later that day, after Amy texted asking whether my adventure had been successful. 'I bought six pairs of undies and somehow lost one between the shop and my house. How? How did that happen?' I said. We spitballed possible locations.

'Maybe under the car seat?' Amy suggested. I searched for them there later that evening, my dog Bosco in the back, waiting patiently for her walk. On one of the few radio stations my car picked up, a panel of people were talking about microwaves.

'Yeah, so two of my flatmates fell in love at a microwave cooking class,' a panellist said. 'They would come home and cook each other microwave dinners.'

Perhaps this is why I'm single, I thought, for even if my microwave hadn't been broken, you couldn't pay me to cook someone a casserole in it.

I stuck my hand down the narrow crevice between the passenger seat and the grubby centre console, pulling out, a few seconds later, only a thick layer of dust and sand. *Possyum*, I thought. *There are probably chunks of Possyum dogroll down there too.*

The following morning Amy messaged again, greeting me as a 'Disposer of Underwear Without a Backward Glance'. I laughed, but I also felt like a fraud. After searching my car I had looked for the undies on the ramp and stairs of my apartment complex, even in the bike rack, as though they may have wheeled themselves there. I searched my apartment, too, wondering if perhaps they had fallen from my arms in the hall and then been kicked in with the laundry or Bosco's toys. Standing above my solid oak drawers, I recounted the new pairs one, two, three times, hoping that I had just missed them, that it had been my arithmetic at fault.

Those undies are gone, though, blowing around the carpark of Outlet City, or perhaps tumbling down the flat streets of Tawa. While I realise it was not the underwear itself but the act of buying it that was important, I can't help but think of the missing pair wistfully. It's not the price that gets me down so much as the value, the opportunity cost. It was $17.95 worth of fabric, sure, but in another life I could have got $80 had I on-sold them worn.

In another life, though, I guess I might not have cared.

MEDB CHARLETON

Stars on Every Lemon Tree

On the lemon tree stars
glow in dark leaves.
This is my divine;
little moon-ends of lunar light

leaking love and rumoured things.
I rest on their pillows.
Tell them I saw kōtuku
at the estuary today.

Too easy to say stars, they sigh.
Too easy to say white.
Too easy to say crinoline skirts
of stars those herons had.

But I can't resist
the dark chase of scent
the pull-in-swift
of petals in sashay.

They turn heads,
these flowers
that make desire
freewheel

then dim their lights
and fade out, fall from grace
leaving behind fruit
like pellets of the known world.

WES LEE

My Mother's Skin

The plane of her breastbone
disappearing under her dress as if it had been ironed.
Pinching the skin on her wrist.
'Chicken skin,' I used to call it
while we both watched it sink. And my flesh
would smooth almost in the time it took
to pinch.
I think of my therapist, Marie,
who would be an old woman now.

KIT WILLETT

Playing with Dolls

I don't remember being told I couldn't,
but I remember the brief moment
when my cousin, five years younger,
left her bedroom to get a snack.

I knew I only had thirty seconds,
maybe less, to reach out a shaking hand,
grasp the muscled body of the second Ken,
and bring their plastic lips together.
After it happened, they never spoke again.

I loved that room, with its pink accent wall
and rainbow stickers on the glass.
The costume bin was full
of make-believe creatures:
men with wings, and parents
who never returned to take me home.

BRETT CROSS

trees

he meets himself in the doorway
him going in him going out

the apartment complex the street
is broad and tree lined, cars

pebble the kerbs, bins sentry
the driveways, go up to the room

where he came from, press open
the tactile door, an apartment

a sofa, a fridge, the aroma
of himself being here

settle into the grooves, search
the clothes-filled drawers

strain in front of the photos
himself going about his farce

tidy up his tracks, carefully
close the door, walk back out

to the street the sentries
the trees that root to the verge

AYESHA GREEN

A Series of Coloured Pencils

1 Coloured Pencils #1
2 Coloured Pencils #2
3 Coloured Pencils #3
4 Coloured Pencils #4
5 Coloured Pencils #5
6 Coloured Pencils #6
7 Coloured Pencils #7
8 Coloured Pencils #9

All coloured pencil on paper, 820 x 610mm, 2023

PENCIL IS AS PENCIL DOES

Witness the act of drawing, how it performs. Watch as the pencil represents itself while caught in the act of representing. In this suite of drawings, Ayesha Green lures us into the performance of drawing itself, asking: what is it to draw, how do we represent the act and how do we create meaning from such an act? The pencils, these small coloured pigments, form a kind of simulacra of themselves, urging us to think about who and what acts upon and constitutes meaning. How does the koru show us its swirl if not through the act of swirling? How does the pencil render meaning if not through a picture of itself making of that same meaning? Pencil is as pencil does, it seems. Or, perhaps in Green's hand, pencil does as pencil is.

— Lynley Edmeades

draw

drawing

drawn

drawing
drawing
drawing
drawing
drawing
drawing
drawing
drawing
drawing
drawing
drawing
drawing
drawing

KIRBY WRIGHT

Make Horse Beach, Moloka'i

FORGET IT. No way you swimmin' out deah. Get ghost o' dat hop-a-long snow stallion dat paniolo wen drag by rope out past da breakahs. No ack. Quit dog-paddlin' da shallows.

On rainy days I heah dat stallion callin' from deep offshore. Stay his neigh-neigh-neigh cry fo' help. Sometimes da waves build and I spock white in da blue—dat ghost lookin' fo' his ridah.

Get black cloud today. Rain comin'. Mo bettah you hele da waddah wiki wiki.

make: dead
paniolo: cowboy
no ack: quit showing off
spock: see
hele: leave
wiki wiki: fast

LORRAINE CARMODY

Denial

And that's the other thing, he said from the edge of the Super King, the pillows three deep, the sheets sea green.

She was faraway, aboard the *Queen Mary*, Singapore to Southampton, thirty-six nights at sea, Southeast Asia, the Suez Canal, the Mediterranean. The sights she'd see! Colombo, Salalah, Cadiz. She'd see them all. Back alleys, and deserts, rainforests with leeches and snakes, cicadas, and shrill, colourful birds. She'd ride in trishaws through crowded streets, and on donkeys bearing crosses, up narrow, winding trails and down. She'd stand on ledges with sheer drops. She'd sit in air-conditioned minivans with leather seats and stare out into the heat, and at her reflection in the tinted windows, and listen to guides telling jokes and anecdotes, and who'd say, you're welcome. She'd tip. She'd take selfies. She'd thumb through her *Lonely Planet*. She'd bookmark chapters. She'd know the best cafés. The best museums to visit. The best of everything. She'd give coins to beggars and chewing gum to children. She'd watch out for pickpockets and con men and other unsavoury types. She'd keep her handbag zipped.

You're not listening, said Dan, turning to face her, looking her straight in the eye.

Yes, I am, she said. I'm listening to every word.

He rolled away from her, taking the top sheet with him, yanking it over his shoulders. It was up to his neck.

For God's sake, Kel, he said.

There's no need to yell, she said.

She lay there and stared at his back, rigid, on the other side of the bed, at the single pillow, a memory foam, under his head, at the other pillows cast aside on the bedroom floor. She turned away from him, moved closer to her edge. There was a big gap between them.

She'd be at sea for days and days. She wouldn't see land, or if she did, just a mirage, an out-of-reach glimpse on the horizon. She'd sit on deckchairs and read books. Maugham, Lawrence, Forster. She'd wear a wide-brimmed straw hat, and round sunglasses, and apply sunscreen every two hours. She'd know her starboard from her port. She'd listen carefully to what the captain would say over the intercom, through the static and the muffle and the rough seas. He'd be Greek. *Yasou*, she'd say to him whenever she passed him on his way to the bridge, her eyes drawn to the stripes on his epaulettes. He'd tilt his head and smile. He'd be tall, olive-skinned, grey at the temples. He'd have kind eyes.

I have something to tell you, Dan said. He turned to face her again. She felt surprisingly calm.

She'd keep a journal to pass the time at sea. The days would be long. The journal would have 2024 written in red, in bold, on the cover. She'd get it from Typo. She'd write in it every day. *Rough sea last night. A bit seasick. Smooth sailing today. Saw captain.* She'd fan her face and take sips from a bottle of mineral water. She'd go to the gym before breakfast. She'd swim in the pool at midday. She'd play roulette after dinner. Drink margaritas. She'd watch sun ups and sun downs.

Dan's voice was low and steady. He'd wanted to tell her for a while, he said.

Go on, she said.

The ship would tread water—blue, green, grey, mile after nautical mile. She'd spend her days mesmerised by the sea's shape, its sound, its unfathomable depth. There'd be storms. High waves. Foam. She'd stand on the deck and feel the spray of the sea running down her face like tears, and taste the salt, bitter, on her lips. She'd keep a tube of ChapStick in her pocket. A tissue handy. She'd peer through tiny binoculars at migrating whales and pods of dolphins and seabirds with broad beaks. A waiter would bring a cup of tea to her deckchair. English Breakfast. There'd be a small biscuit—shortbread, or chocolate chip, or a macaroon (pink)—on the saucer. She'd eat it whole.

Say something, said Dan, anything at all.

She cleared her throat, opened her mouth, but there were no words.

She thought of the clothes she'd need. She'd make a list. A long list. She needed to get it right. She'd memorise the list, store it, unpack it whenever she needed it. It would take some time to put together. Some thought. It would be a long voyage. So she began.

T-shirts (seven)
Red dress
White dress
Grey dress (short one)
Shorts (five)
Togs (how many?)
Trousers, light (three)
Cardigan (one)
Umbrella
Sandals
Jandals
Lime shoes
Straw hat
Ballgown (blue)

The bedside clock blinked. It was 01.07. On the other side of the bed Dan was snoring. He was tangled in the sheets. She didn't say, *wake up, turn over, you're making a bit of a ruckus there, Dan*, or even shake him like she usually would have. She lay still and stared at him, at his strange familiarity. His face, so well known, was on the backs of buses and motorway billboards and in weekend newspapers. Dan, the brand, the slogan (*Looking out for People*), an image, who stood out purposefully with his red ties—spotted, striped, paisley—and his whitened teeth, who looked like he played golf every other weekend. He was a realtor.

She'd dine at the captain's table. She'd be one of a group of eight, French, Germans, Brazilians, sitting around a circular table with a soft, flickering candle in the centre. She'd wear her blue ballgown. It would show off the colour of her eyes. The captain would tell her this when he leaned closer. She'd sip champagne. Eat foie gras. Caviar. The band would start playing and the captain would ask her to dance. My name is Nico, he'd say. He'd be a widower (two years now).

She'd always known Dan. They'd married when he was twenty-one, she nineteen. It was expected. They were from the same place, Hei Hei, a suburb on the outskirts, treeless, ringed by transition towers carrying electricity to other places. Kel and her mother lived next door to the Samoan church; Dan and his, around the corner from KFC. Other kids were drawn to him. Dan had the gift of the gab even then, said Kel's mother.

Neither had siblings, nor fathers. They had that in common. Her father was somewhere up north, his in Australia, in the mines, making big money, his mother said. Every Christmas he sent Dan a present. A plastic tip-truck, a Wallabies junior rugby ball, a XXXX beer t-shirt when he was twelve, a stubby holder (Tooheys) at fifteen. Hers never sent anything.

She'd play table tennis and paddle tennis (it was in the itinerary) and minigolf on the *Queen Mary*. She'd be a good sport. She'd sit still. She'd hum hymns. She'd listen to the pianist, and the harpist, and the string trio. She'd drink pink gin from a bulbous glass. She'd watch magic shows and dance performances and aerial acrobats and illusionists swallowing swords and fire, and she'd laugh out loud at stand-up comedians and clap and cheer variety entertainers, and concentrate when she went to the mid-afternoon Shakespearian plays.

When she and Dan were newlyweds they bought an old railway house, two bedrooms, wooden, opposite the fertiliser factory on the main road. They got it for a song. Kel cleaned the windows every week, inside and out, to keep the factory's sediment, a yellow dust, from settling. They replaced the rotting window frames with aluminium. Dan watered the lawn on Saturdays, although the grass took some coaxing. Kel put the rubbish bin out on Friday mornings. They kept the windows shut to stop the odour, a sharp, medicinal smell, from penetrating and their eyes smarting. She worried about deformed babies. They were surprised a couple of years later when they sold the place and made a profit. That's when Dan decided to move into real estate.

Nico would be from Paros or Naxos or possibly Corfu. He'd have a white house in the country, near a village, on top of a hill overlooking the sea. It would be at the end of a winding road, surrounded by an olive grove. Nico would grow grapes. He'd drink Retsina. He'd hold a string of worry beads in his hand. Whenever he was close by she'd hear the rhythmic clack, clack, clack of them. His elderly mother, who kept a goat or two, would live nearby. He'd check on her every day.

After they sold the railway house, she and Dan moved a few kilometres south from Hei Hei into the country, to a village, as the locals called it—a foreign-sounding word to Kel and Dan. They pinched themselves. They'd bought a peeling-stucco, three-bedroom house opposite a mushroom farm that was undergoing expansion. Kel got a job in the sheds picking mushrooms—white buttons, brown flats. The sheds were humid. She wore a t-shirt right throughout winter. Her hair, usually straight, grew fashionably curly. It suits you, said Dan, running his fingers through the strands.

 The farm got bigger and bigger and the smell—like old sweat—grew more unpleasant and pungent, particularly on those foggy winter mornings when there was no wind to speak of. She and Dan both shrugged. They were used to unsavoury smells. They kept their windows closed and looked away, beyond the sheds to the view of the paddocks with sheep and pine shelterbelts, trimmed in autumn, and the snow on the alps in winter. They were happy. Kel got promoted to the packing shed, and then to the office. She showed a lot of promise, her boss said.

 There was a hue and cry. The locals in the village wanted to be able to open their sliding doors on weekends and fire up the barbecue and have a few beers and a sauvignon blanc outside without having to hold their noses or dry retch. A committee was formed. Dan joined it. He sensed the mood, he said to Kel.

 The committee drew up a roster and took turns to protest with placards outside the mushroom farm gate. Stop the Pong. They did the same at the council service centre. The mayor accused the protesters of being anti-progress, NIMBYs, wannabes with an axe to grind, Johnny-come-latelys even. It stung. The committee chairman resigned and Dan put his hand up for the job. He was interviewed by the local newspaper. Local Real Estate Agent Against Foul Stench. It was front-page news. Dan was eloquent, they said in the village. A born leader. He sold more houses. He was on the TV news. Kel was pregnant, four months gone with Jace, when she got sacked from the farm.

 Nico would invite her to stay in his house on the hill. She'd sip Metaxa and Ouzo and eat olives and stuffed vine leaves and Nico's mother's homemade feta. She'd sit on the verandah and put her feet up. She'd take deep breaths. The sun would stream down on her. She'd be able to smell the sea.

 The council forced the mushroom farm to move out. The village expanded, and when the motorway was built, the place really took off. More people moved in. Land was opened up for development. A new school was built. A roundabout put in. A set of traffic lights. The place was no longer a village.

Dan and Kel painted the stucco and sold it (another profit) and bought a one-hectare block, with a four-bedroom spec and a three-car garage. They sold that and bought another house and another. By the time Jace had grown and left home they were in a five-bed, architecturally designed brick, with a pool and a hot tub and a horseshoe driveway. The décor was minimalist. Dan didn't like clutter. They seldom visited Hei Hei.

Dan had a big team behind him now. Responsibilities. Worries. A white Maserati to clean at weekends. He wore expensive aftershave (Dior Sauvage Elixir) and Gucci shoes without visible socks. He had a personal assistant with blonde hair and long legs and a butterfly tattoo on her left wrist. Her name was Cassandra. She was closer in age to Jace than Dan. Dan said he didn't know what he'd ever do without Cassandra in his life.

Kel would have a cabin with an ocean view, and a balcony to step onto in the evenings. She'd take deep breaths. When she'd lean over the rail and turn her face towards the bridge she'd be able to see it gleaming in the fading light.

Back inside the cabin she'd ring room service and ask for an Americano. A waiter would bring it to her on a silver tray. She'd add a liqueur. Cointreau, or Kahlua, or Campari. Or all of them. She'd keep a bottle of each in her cabin.

She'd open the wardrobe door and take out the complimentary white robe and slippers. She'd undress and put on the robe, slip her bare feet into the slippers. She'd throw her shoes willy-nilly across the room. She'd drip coffee down the front of the robe. She'd leave her discarded clothes lying on the cabin floor.

CRAIG FOLTZ

Petroglyph

We rely on markers to distinguish between species. The scent of a freshly hewn peach. The sound of iron rods & brass cords. Membrane-bound organelles & their associated subsets. Someone keeps us warm with fire.

We used to hoard pamphlets & other seditious materials, but turned them over to the authorities in order to pursue collective structures & other morphology. Dander vs dandruff. Flying fox vs Four Square. Indeed. Viral vs bacterium.

A small pellet of coloured sugar.

Oh, to feel the gentle tug of taxonomies! Oh, to understand morbidity through sentient epidemiology! But then again. Some of us here cannot abandon the broad consensus of decontextualised abstraction. Bunkers in unexpected locations, tender Sandusky. Some of us cannot map the terrain of these transactional alliances. Nor choose between flavours of irony. Cardamom. Cashmere. Calendula.

Petroglyph

Turns out, the epiphany was not an epiphany at all, but was born from a lack of sleep & a landscape bereft of dreams. Strangers describe the difference between rain & rainfall. Rainfall & periodicals. Periodicals & footnotes. They use their limbs to perforate the blossoms formed by a hoop of delicate wire or by a simple mesh of fingers. Parsing translates loosely.

Petroglyph

One of us takes the form of a small child whose eyes have enlarged with higher rod densities in order to capture images of bioluminescence. We crave objects that are brand new, but then treat these things as if they are invisible.

Another is an even smaller child whose mineral axis is covered in an array of colours so bewildering that they become the dominant paradigm. He takes the form of one animal after another (turtle, peacock, cheetah), but cannot settle on which.

Then there is another one, who maintains a youthful outlook by dragging a miniature version of herself around behind us wherever she goes. This miniature version has pigtails & carries a deck of cards in the back pocket of their jeans. She says, *I have followed you from a place of light to a place of dark. I have held myself together with long-extinct memories of who I used to be.*

CONNIE BUCHANAN

The Tōtara at 14 Stanley

These days it's an urban tree. A city has come up around it. Within its compass are twenty-one houses, a kindergarten, one set of shops, a park and a swimming school. If it were to fall in any direction, at any time, a person might get crushed.

Whoever owned 14 Stanley Street technically owned the tree. When the previous lot moved in, the woman stood under it, holding up her phone to the stiff pointed little leaves and then to the shaggy bark.

'Oh right,' she muttered, looking at the screen. 'A tōtara. Of *course*.'

She had to crank her head right back to see the crown. The trunk was huge, thick with branches and leaves all the way up, a vigorous old king in a bristling robe, massively out of proportion to the brown front door of the green house.

Next door on one side were retired Judith and David Stack. The tōtara filled their side window. Through the glass, David sat in his comfortable chair while Judith talked continuously at him from the kitchen as she peeled and stewed Granny Smiths. Twice a day she swept the beige hexagons of the vinyl flooring she'd chosen in 1975, never replaced after a builder told them the hexagons were reinforced with asbestos and trebled his quote.

Next door on the other side were the Ricketts, who kept their cars in the front yard, their dogs in the back yard, and their guns in the master bedroom. In summer the tōtara threw shade on the adult son, Anton, when he had his bonehead mates over. They did bombs off the shed roof into a round plastic pool which stuck up above the ground. They took long pulls from brown bottles as they climbed and jumped. Simon Taylor at number 14 hoped that one day one of them would misjudge it. Instead of ba-*boom* ba-*boom* into the pool—doing his bloody head in as he tried to sip a single malt in peace—it'd be ba-*oh fuck*. Then, fingers crossed, the wail of sirens.

*

The tōtara's main gig was to overlook the front yard of number 14, where it supervised the three Taylor boys, Hunter, Henry and Hugo. Loud and running, slamming in and out of the front door, they fired their fingers at each other, sliced the air with sticks, biffed lemons onto the roof, released arcs of pee against the fence.

Once the youngest tried to build a hut with branches and a cardboard box. One of the older ones arrived to sneer at the project. He smashed a football around the yard, driving it into the fence over and over, then right over, straight through the side window and onto David Stack's corduroy lap in a shower of glass.

The tōtara oversaw the quivering apology. It monitored another more serious one when the adult son on the other side somehow shot his dad's gun through the kitchen window of number 14. Police responded fast to the furious call from Simon Taylor, and the middle Taylor boy hurtled out the front door when he heard the knock, ahead of his red-faced father.

'It was the bogans next door that did it!' he yelled, and the main cop, the impressive one with the pistol and the biceps, laughed.

'I reckon you're right, buddy,' she said as she peered through the bullet's entry hole. Half-cooked pancakes sat on the stove, the congealed rounds dimpled and crunchy with glass.

The tōtara was the only witness when the tall window by the brown front door was smashed in. All three boys made their eyes go wide and said, 'What? What are you talking about, Dad? What window? Where? What cricket bat?'

All this glass was merely a teaspoon of sand in a tree's lifetime but it spelled the end. The family wanted more space. They called a real estate agent with expensive teeth, who in turn called a developer of apartments, who in turn called his backers, the ones with plenty of yuan who remained bullish about the market for medium-density housing.

Everyone on all sides made sure to check about the tree. Was it protected? Could they get rid of it? Would the wonks at the council kick up a fuss?

There were 350 protected trees on the council's Schedule 9D, ranked according to a standard valuation system. The tōtara's points added up to not enough. It was not one of the special 350. This seemed strange for such a big old native but there you go, shrugged the agent, picking a dark thread off his pale linen jacket. Yes, it could be taken down to make way for apartments.

Yes, it could be hacked to bits, wrenched up from the roots like an enormous resistant tooth.

'What a relief, that's great!' everyone said.

*

Autumn arrived. The kindy kids were delighted when the tree with the fruit that smelled like spew started dropping it all over their playground. It *stinks!* they screamed. They stuck orange paper ribbons and autumn leaves on their tricycles and rode around the block, past the tōtara, waving to one another, waving to the tree, waving to the ants. One last regatta before the cold weather set in.

*

Judith and David were astonished at the sale price, reported to them over the fence by Simon. Judith said 'I'm gobsmacked' three times in a row.

'We rattle around a bit at ours nowadays, don't we?' she said to David, who pointed out that the place needed a new roof as well as a new floor. Was it worth it when their back yard was big enough for apartments too?

Judith turned out to be the brisk and unsentimental one, filling skip after skip with the clutter of forty years. It was David who pawed through the piles, rescuing a dress their daughter had worn as a toddler, and an oil painting of a boiling blue lake pierced by a fork of lightning, scrawled with their son's signature at the bottom.

'The only thing I'm really sad about is leaving the tree,' Judith said. 'I loved waking up and looking out the window and seeing it there.'

The market shifted. The apartment plan for number 14 got put on hold. The investors rented out the green house to an engineering student, a computer science major, a barista and a junior council staffer while their backers re-did the calculations. The investors, now reluctant landlords, decided to push ahead with taking down the tōtara, clearing the way for when the market recovered. They booked the cheapest tree man they could find.

*

What a wanker the tree man turned out to be.

'You're a wanker,' Hayden the barista said, as he concluded their chat on the doorstep. The tree man said he had his gear in the truck. Hayden said they'd had no notification. There was a flat party about to start. An execution, even partial, would wreck the vibe. The three other flatmates hooted and cheered him on in the background.

The party went ahead. As it started pumping, they invented a drinking game called Cockwomble to celebrate getting rid of the tree man. At one point very early the next morning the four flatmates joined hands around the tōtara's trunk and slurred into the brown bark that they would protect her for ever and ever, amen.

On Monday they rang the landlord to say stop sending tradies without telling us, we have rights. The landlord rebooked the tree man for three weeks' time and said get it in your calendar this time, you lot.

Mitch, the flatmate who had a job in the wastewater division of the council, brought home copies of information pertinent to the tree. He read sections aloud in a voice so toneless the others could not absorb what he was saying:

> One of the challenges for effective biodiversity conservation in highly modified landscapes is efficiently finding sites with the greatest potential to represent the historic ecosystem pattern.

'Give it here,' said Eddie, and snatched the printout, reading it to himself with his lips moving. 'Right. So basically, because our gorgeous Brown Beauty is only her own stunning self and not part of a blah blah blah, she can be destroyed.'

The mission came together fast. They actually wore balaclavas on the night they used Mitch's swipe card to sneak into council offices. Two kept watch at the doors, one tried to stick an arm up the vending machine, and Eddie got to work hacking the back end of the tree points system. He made minute adjustments, double-checked the new rankings, then retraced his digital prints, erasing and scrubbing step by backward step. On the way home, Mitch tossed his swipe card into the river. Made sure to moan at work the next week about the hassle of a stolen wallet. Then it was just a matter of a phone call impersonating the landlord, and a request confirmed in writing.

The Robbins moved in to number 14 Stanley Street next. Their teenage daughter, Paige, often arranged herself on a plastic deckchair in the front garden, waiting for the swimming school instructors to walk past shirtless on their way to work. She ate apples in massive chomps like a pony, sometimes looking at her book, more often picking up her phone to contribute to a sustained campaign of bullying against Emily Ding.

Summer crawled in around her. Fingers of weedy green pushed through the established growth. When the sun beat down too harshly on her screen, Paige got up and stood beneath the shade of the tōtara. It tolerated her sweating back pressed into the bark, its sap still fluid and rising.

ZOË MEAGER

I was born crooked

Always looking down at the ground. *What're ya lookin' for?* People always say.

Twenny dollars. I dropped my twenny dollars and that's it till benefit day.

Aw, sucks, people say, or sometimes, *Sucks to be you,* and if they're weird (like nuns or new mums, or girls who do well in school), they'll help me look.

My chest tightens just thinking of the made-up twenny dollars that'll never be found. *Had it right here,* I pat my breast pocket, trying to calm my heart, *had it right here and then POOF!*

And all of them start looking (the shop girls and the office girls and lady with her arm in a sling), all of them bent over, scouring the ground, all of them saying so nicely, *It could've flown off in the wind,* because that seems true to them; that bad luck in life is just as fleeting as the wind.

REBECCA BALL

all our warmth and colour

we paint our plates with grease drink wine instead of water
let kiwifruit dissolve in the fruit bowl as if we could

beckon those cells from their body press them bubbling to
our flesh hold them under the skin to breed we look

into cold mirrors search our lower lids for paleness check
our tongues for ulcers pray for lumps for nausea remain

resolutely alive

hair bursting slick from our heads fat gathering in plumes
around our waists blood pumping in vibrant protest

in our hands we turn to sprouting grains to dusty kūmara
slice split fill steel pots with broth bubble it for days our

houses fill with steam and spice sinks tight with bowls
Tupperware stacked like apartments in the freezer our

tiny town in the snow all our warmth and colour stirred up
cooked down packed tight sealed against the cold

CLAIRE ORCHARD

The best bird for your return

There is an argument to be made
for the laidback lifestyle of the ruru,
perched high in a hollow section
of macrocarpa trunk on the fence line,
calling for more pork while
chowing down on freshly caught gecko.
But the dawn chorus of well-off farmers
harping on about the evils of non-existent
wealth taxes would quickly get old.
People will say eagle. And sure,
the one charged with pecking out the liver
of poor, dumb Prometheus would mean
all you can eat, at least until along comes
Hercules. No one wants to be a city pigeon—
so disparaged and despised—but some
will argue the nobility of a country kererū.
I toyed with the idea of a dove, but there's
weddings and funerals to consider, also
occasional magicians with their hard hands,
their tangled strings of brightly coloured scarves.
A resplendent, salmon-pink flamingo,
elegant among an assembly of tropical birds
in an imagined utopian landscape sounds fine
until a troop of homeless hoiho show up
and awkwardly stand around. No,
hands down the best bird for your return
is a peacock, perched with panache upon
an ornate garden urn. Oh, to be a peacock
atop a decorative urn, now the 17th century is here.

SCOTT MENZIES

The Lovely Boys

The one to Colin's left, the blonde, he's had a haircut since he saw him yesterday. The hairline is precise, like the edge of the grass along the paths after the old man cut them. His eyes caress the pearl-white slopes between blonde's crisp shirt collar and freshly cropped hair and savour the freckle like an island on the sea of honey-coloured flesh below the not-quite-tamed curls of his black-haired companion.

They always sit together, the lovely boys. They're not skinny, and they're not fat; they're just big enough that their shoulders and sides and—as Colin has seen with glances as he edges past their seat—their thighs press against each other. He wonders if they get on at the same stop. He's not so obsessed that he's gotten up early and taken a bus to the start of the route to check, but he's thought about it. He wonders if they live together, if they eat their breakfast together, leave the house together. They can't be older than twenty-five.

He thinks of Carey, that piss-up at somebody's flat back in 1985. Colin and Carey had been friends since they were nippers. They and a couple of mates had chipped in for a crate of jars. And the lounge in the old villa with the high ceiling and bay window reeked of pot and cigarettes.

At the end of the night everyone else had stumbled to their cars or their rooms. Carey plonked down on the sofa beside him.

'You've got eyes like paua shells,' he said around his cigarette. He reached out and touched Colin's leg.

'Stop it,' Colin said.

Carey leaned over, his lips puckered.

Colin pushed him away, hard. 'Get off, you poof!'

Carey looked confused. Then he sneered.

Colin leapt from the sofa and staggered to the veranda. His mind reeled. He thought to be a poof you had to be like Hudson and Halls or Mr Humphries, or a dirty old perve like the one who groped him at the Westend

Cinema that time. Not a normal guy like Carey. It knocked him for six.

It knocked them apart, too. They didn't speak to each other after that night. They saw each other all the time because they were part of the same bunch of punks, but they didn't speak.

★

Colin lowers his gaze from the lovely boys on the bus. He sees Vogel, the name of the seat manufacturer, stamped in grey plastic. Vogel is the German word for bird, which is funny because how many birds across the country eat Vogel's bread? He splashed out on a loaf once. He ripped half of it up and scattered it across the backyard and laughed as he watched the starlings and blackbirds eat it. His mum, a stubborn old chook, she turned her nose up at it, told him white bread is good enough for her.

Sir Julius Vogel. He bets no one else on the bus has heard of him. People should though. He doesn't know if he's related to the bread people but he knows he wrote New Zealand's first science fiction story. In the story, Sir Julius predicted women would be as powerful as men by the year two thousand and he was right. Sir Julius was premier of New Zealand twice. The Americans are always making movies and TV shows about their presidents, but you never see anything like that about our premiers and prime ministers, which is a shame because some of them are bloody interesting, like Sir Julius Vogel.

About. There's a word on its last legs. These days people say *around* when they should say *about*. He hears it all the time and it gets on his wick. I have questions *around* this, they say, or we'll come up with a plan *around* this. Let's talk *around* it, his shrink had said. Sure he could, Colin had said, but wouldn't it be better to talk *about* it? *Around* means to avoid something, as in walk around it. It did when he went to school anyway. There's that episode of The Twilight Zone where a guy starts noticing radio announcers and his family swapping words around, and only he notices it. Colin reckons some idiot in a suit somewhere started saying *around* instead of *about* and everyone's followed him, like sheep.

Shit. He's forgotten his gloves. He's getting as bad as his mum. He looks at his hands. Arthritic, wrinkled. Christ, these hands. Stop your grizzling, his mum says, when he curses over them. Thank your stars you're not like your

Uncle Harry, she says. He lost his right hand at the workshops in Addington. His mates made a claw that fitted over his stump so he could hold onto things, like a glass or a bottle. He was a character, Uncle Harry. He used to piggyback Mum around to whatever house they were at for Christmas dinner, half-cut on Wards ale and Mum's cheeks glowing from cherry brandy. But he must've grizzled sometimes. Hell, how could he look at that stump every day and not? People have different ways of grizzling, of course. Never saw Uncle Harry sober.

The bus climbs the bridge over the railway. He looks east, through bright dust on the window, at the tracks stretching off to the port.

*

Carey got a shiner in a fight outside the Star and Garter. Colin had watched from the sidelines. He can't remember how it kicked off. The punks and the beeries were always kicking off at that shithole. Carey's cigarette went flying.

Carey gave up being a punk after that fight. He grew his hair and stopped wearing the metal studded wristbands and the denim jacket. He went right out of Colin's life. Colin often wondered about him. Heard he lived with a wharfie for a while.

As the bus pulls into the exchange, the lovely boys rise from their perch. For months Colin has watched them get off, inch their way down the aisle, pass through the sliding door to a chorus of thank yous to the driver, and vanish. His stop isn't for a while yet but he finds himself standing and getting off the bus, and the blonde one and his mate, they're going out the main entrance and he's following them.

It wasn't legal back then, that night on the sofa with Carey. You could get done for being a poof. You could go to prison. Who wanted to be marked for life as a poof on the Wanganui Computer? He ended up on it anyway but not for that.

He zips his jacket higher and reminds himself they can't see inside him, they can't hear his thoughts, just like the shrink couldn't unless he told them out loud, and he's never been good at that.

There are so many young people on the streets, new and shiny like the buildings around here now, which are nothing like the motley lot they've replaced, all knocked down, that had the bars for the shy boys and the coy boys, upstairs and downstairs, through anonymous doors that were invisible to most people. Colin saw Carey in those bars once. They didn't speak. Carey was with another guy and they looked happy together, and that knocked Colin for six, too.

The lovely boys are striding north, two, three, four, five. At Cashel Street, they pause. Colin stops next to a pillar. Its base is surrounded by bird shit and the word is it's never scrubbed away to stop it being used as a begging spot. The blonde one kisses his mate on the lips.

Colin's heart clutches. He steadies himself against the pillar.

He may as well walk to Merivale Mall from here. Hopefully, some dropkick hasn't binned the square of cardboard he leaves on his spot near the mall door. He could make forty bucks today if the sun entices local matrons, local pink dollars and their canine controllers. He could stop at the tavern and shout his mum tea. His sign reads *Bet you one dollar you'll read this.*

'The Lovely Boys' is published in memory of Scott Menzies, 3/5/1974–27/2/2024.

MIKAELA NYMAN

Mudlarking

Each bend and flat tells a different story: prehistoric flints,
bone hair pins, dainty bone dice and counters

Bronze Age pots, copper nails dropped from countless ships.
Reminds us of the thousands that died in the Great Stink of 1858.

A rubbish dump for millennia, a giant sewer, tidal Thames yields
its archived secrets.

Miles and miles of mudflats, boggy
treacherous. How deep, no one knows. Still tidal.

⋆

Tilbury saw the Windrush generation blow in from Jamaica,
skylarkers and ten pound poms depart for our shores.

Feel the imprints of toes in leather, perfectly preserved,
as if this small medieval child lost her shoe only yesterday.

Skulls and bones from convicts awaiting deportation, Napoleon's
Prisoners of War upon their unlucky return

found and sold to glue merchants.
None of them afforded a decent burial.

Declared technically and biologically dead in the 1950s this body
of water now boasts 125 species of fish, oysters, lobster and salmon.

A small miracle right there.

⋆

Meanwhile, we're creating our own Great Stink right here
forcing iwi to place a rāhui over the Mimitangiatua Awa

leaching   into root and leaf
leaching   into fish and molluscs

the health and mauri of the awa at stake—
    Do not gather and eat kai from this water.
    Do not swim here.

NATHANIEL CALHOUN

below the graft

something parked shades something living
into damp carbon. eucalyptus carpet bombs
untended fertile earth.

a dusty diorama of old goals:
talcum catching in little joints,
locked jaws, an inner cohort tottering
stilted by reminiscence.
mould smells old but comes quickly.

the pledge to assemble
a sensory array capable of holding
two hearts together got
baked into a cookie and
given to whomever.

some find the ceremony of caring
tedious. some become volcanoes.
others walk the shore after storm
their hounds in search of ambergris.

wildflower seeds in the wrong packet
bloom perfectly suited to indelible moments—
and get marked all over with red pen.

a tree nursed from seed until it fruits
turns out to come from stock
below the graft—
worthless to the palette.

CINDY BOTHA

Geraniums

I told him I longed for a dress
the colour of geraniums
and he said *I don't know what that is,*
stared at me when I said *red,*
it's just red, mumbled
you always use fancy words
trying to sound smart
which wasn't a question

so I didn't answer,
didn't point out the blooms
when he passed them headed
for the street,
little meteors in the quivering dusk,
the bushes holding their breath,
but as he drove away
the flowers hummed and flared.

HARVEY MOLLOY

A singer returns

(News item: Hip priest lamas have confirmed the reincarnation of Mark E. Smith in Dunedin.)

When the black caped monks came they wanted to be sure
I was taken to a basement cluttered with bric-a-brac
boaters, banjoes, bangles from Bangalore
amongst the distractions his treasured mementos
the snow globe he shook each day, a videocassette of Zulu,
dark brown bottles of fortified milk stout, Can's *Ege Bamyasi*,
each I identified with three taps of my nail.

At the rock monastery I took to cartooning
grotesque caricatures of my teachers and classmates
I would break from the course they had charted for me
I wouldn't sing, scrawl in a notebook, smoke, or take speed
I would lie fast in the dark in my thought palace fortress
but this defiance they took as another sure sign
any day now my cocoon would crack, ukulele at hand
three chord charms would wing from my slack scarlet mouth.

Making Space

IN COLLABORATION WITH RMIT UNIVERSITY'S non/fictionLab

This series is a collaborative essayistic project, where writers from both sides of the Tasman were invited to work together on the topic of 'making space'. As editors, we were interested to hear how a conversational, trans-Tasman approach might shine a light on the new wave of essays currently being written in Aotearoa and Australia, and to make space in these pages for this kōrero.

Each of the three essays presented here offers a singular and challenging response to the topic. Mia-Francesca Jones and Lauren Vargo's essay meditates on the ramifications of the earth's process of making space through a sensitive observation of glacial melt and climate change. In 'Repoeming', Airini Beautrais and Jessica L. Wilkinson take a close reading of their own poetic practice to consider how documentary poetry can be a space in which to iteratively address difficult historical and biographical material. And finally, Amy Brown and Joan Fleming's 'Affidamento' invites us into the intimacy of the writers' epistolary relationship as they consider the space made and unmade by the decision to have or not have children amid environmental collapse.

At a time when border regimes and isolationist politics are on the rise, collaboration feels like a quiet resistance. We extend this invitation to the reader so that together we might continue to make space—for diversity, community and meaningful connection.

—Lynley Edmeades & Brigid Magner

This is the first installation of the series, which will continue in Landfall 248.

MIA-FRANCESCA JONES & LAUREN VARGO

The Earth Will Be Fine

1: Melting

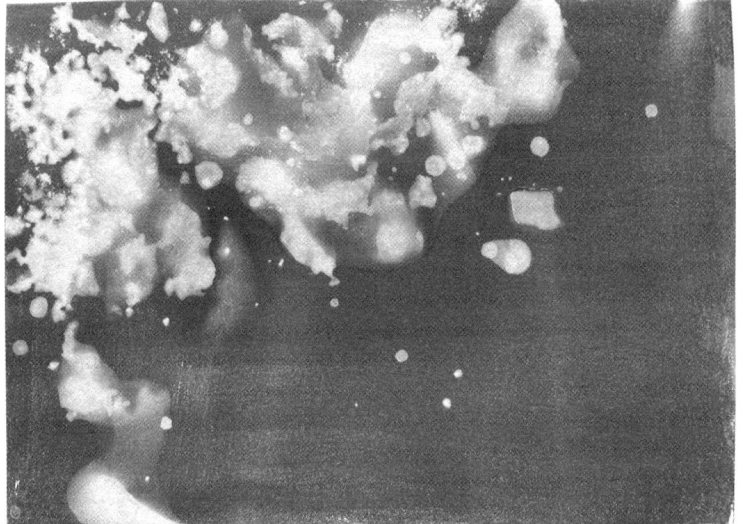

Cyanotype 1: scraped glacier ice on paper, Gulkana glacier, Alaska, June 2022 (Lauren Vargo)

A spark pings across the ocean to connect two computers and two researchers—a scientist and a writer. This connection, facilitated by underwater fibre optic cables, takes a fraction of a second, yet the subject of our inquiry—ice—moves in slow motion.

When I first connected with glaciologist Dr Lauren Vargo over Zoom, I asked her if there was any ice at the Antarctic Research Centre, where she is based in Wellington. She said, *No, it's just a bunch of offices with people studying volcanoes, some rocks, oh—and a mummified penguin in a glass case.* I also asked her advice on visiting one of Aotearoa's glaciers, and she guided me towards Haupapa/Tasman Glacier for its accessibility. Other glaciers, she advised me, had retreated so far that while you used to be able to walk right out onto them, you'd now need to take a helicopter to reach the ice.

I was reading Anne Carson's 'The Glass Essay' at the time, in which the author uses glass and ice as metaphors for fragility, fragmentation and reflection. In 'The Glass Essay', things are always in motion: the protagonist herself, who has just broken up with her boyfriend, travelling by train to her mother's house in the north of Canada, wind that *drifts from the pale sun* and *crops of ice changing to mud*. But the lonely moors surrounding Carson's mother's house are *paralysed with ice*.

Glaciers—flowing masses of ice—exist in this tension between stillness and movement. The impermanence of ice and the instability of glaciers are why a climate scientist and a writer might turn to them to convey a message, that human activity and rising temperatures are leading to the loss of such spaces.

We had been discussing these issues for several months, Lauren and I, about how and why the ice is melting and what it means to our different disciplines, to the climate, and to our personal stories. I was undertaking a movement of my own, travelling from the Victorian goldfields to Wellington, a city so windy that people clap when the plane lands safely on the runway. Following our digital dialogue, we met face-to-face in the middle of summer at The Lab, a coffee shop at Te Herenga Waka Victoria University of Wellington. The university is located on a shoulder of land that is also the site of a historic cemetery. We shared coffee and muffins with the pigeons and fruit flies that blew in through the automatic glass doors while discussing our impending expeditions: to Haupapa/Tasman Glacier in Aoraki/Mount Cook and a trio of glaciers on Mount Ruapehu.

Aoraki's dual name is the result of a 1998 treaty settlement that recognises Māori place names—like Aotearoa. These traditional names are inherently more descriptive of a place and its distinct ecological features than the colonial versions, which are generally named after a person (usually a man). Haupapa is the Māori word for frost and ice and serves as a geographical descriptor for the glacier itself. The ice that carves off the glacier melts into the cloudy lake and then flows into the Mackenzie Basin, which is named after the Dutch pioneer, explorer and sheep thief.

As Rebecca Solnit writes in the *Encyclopedia of Trouble and Spaciousness*, one who sets out on an expedition 'sets out to accomplish, discover, claim, explore. Sets out with an agenda. Sets out often to fail, to get lost, to suffer—'.[1] Writing an essay is like an expedition, the goal of which is to discover, expand and explore, and often involves trial and error, getting lost down a rabbit hole, and enduring some suffering as it spirals back to the heart of the subject. Sidonie Smith and Julia Watson define the personal essay as a form of 'self-exploration', or 'a testing ('assay') of one's own intellectual, emotional, and physiological responses to a given topic'.[2] Expeditions and essays begin with a problem to overcome. We started with this: *How do various disciplines interpret space? Can we prevent glacial retreat? What ecological and narrative voids will emerge in a post-ice era?* Untangling these concepts is a form of exploration.

In January 2024, Lauren led ten selected teenage girls to a glacier as part of an equity programme. The goal of the programme is to foster an interest in snow, science and ice, and address gender disparity in the field of geological sciences. She also undertakes annual expeditions to the South Island's Brewster Glacier to measure glacial melt, using mixed methods of field observations, remote sensing data, climate reanalysis data, GCM output, and numerical modelling. My expedition is more personal, travelling with my young daughter to Haupapa/Tasman Glacier before it disappears completely— visiting Aotearoa's glaciers has been described as 'last chance tourism'.

Lauren is originally from Ohio, a landscape flattened by an ice sheet 20,000 years ago, and I'm from the far North Queensland tropics that drip with humidity year-round. To ground ourselves in these other, at times, problematised spaces—The Lab, Wellington, Aotearoa, the ice—we reflect on the places we've come from. I ask Lauren: If home was a tree, what would it be? If home was an animal, what would it be? *An oak. A deer.* I respond: A palm tree. A curlew.

I pull up a video on my phone so we can listen to the curlew bird's distinct high-pitched call, which sounds like a woman screaming or a baby crying. In local lore, it is the sound of the dead returning to the dreaming and represents the end of something. *Seeing deer in a meadow or a forest,* says Lauren, *can make you feel as though you're a part of a bigger, interconnected thing.* But there is an underlying tension with the creatures that run in front of cars or eat the flowers on the lawn.

Her descriptions of deer remind me of Erika Howsare, the writer who set out on a literary expedition to uncover the role that deer play in the world. One of her methods was to set up an alert for headlines about the animals—*Deer seen flying through the skies in Utah. Woman gored by mule deer buck in front yard*—revealing them as spiritual guides and pests, trophies and intruders. I think about place, too, about what makes a space a place: the stories, mythologies, memories, imaginaries, ecologies, geologies and biologies. *Place* is an extension of *space*.

In 'The Glass Essay', Carson attaches loss and lament to the solid ground of the frozen moors. Bits of gold weed etch themselves to the bottom of the ice, spelling out messages of warning. These icy associations deliver a setting for bad dreams, the silence of grief, and fragmented relationships. The word *ice* is hidden inside the body of other words in the work—*voice, practice, slice, justice, price*—we uncover the role of ice in literature as we read. *When you walk across a glacier*, says Lauren, *the crampons strapped to your shoes leave tiny indents in the ice.* What space, what marks, are left behind in the place of a vanishing glacier? What processes underlie the forming, and melting, of these mountains made of ice?

2: Field notes

Haupapa Glacier is a four-hour drive from east to southwest. I am driving to Lake Ohau first, an off-season ski town that is in the process of being rebuilt after the worst wildfires in Aotearoa's living memory. I prepare to leave my husband and eighteen-month-old daughter in a wooden cabin on the very edge of the lake, and, as always, my daughter doesn't want me to go and clings tightly to my legs. Her father peels her off and takes her out the back door of the cabin to distract her with the mountain and the birds. The road out of Lake Ohau is singular and goes for what feels like forever. There is nothing in the distance but rolling brown hills and cows. I feel anxious leaving them behind with no car, few neighbours besides the two old men sawing and hammering the frame of a house, the fear of fire closing in on them. On the side of the highway to Aoraki there are piles of blackened trees that have been cut, collected and stacked, laid on top of each other like charred bodies. The entire valley of Aoraki was once filled with ice, reaching almost sixty kilometres to the town of Twizel, stretching two hundred metres above ground and four hundred beneath.

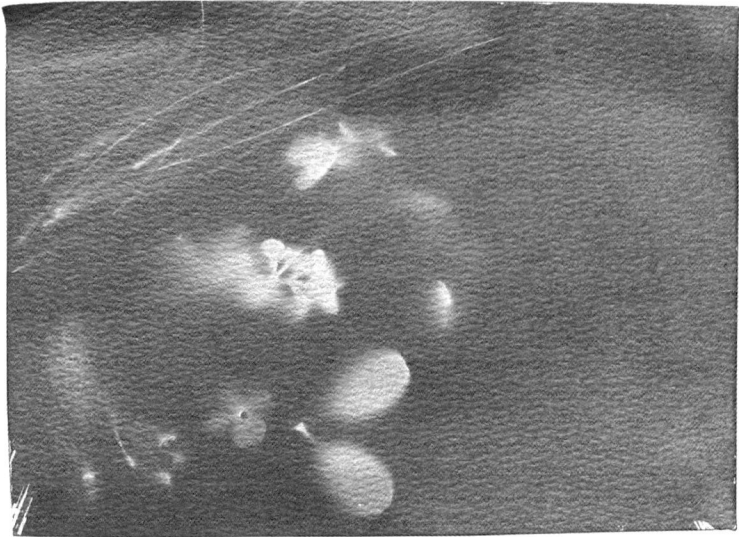

Cyanotype 2: alpine flowers and grasses on paper, Mt Ruapehu, January 2024 (Lauren Vargo)

To get to Haupapa, I drive one hour from Lake Ohau to the National Park, another twenty-five minutes on a bus, a thirty-minute hike through the mountains to the mouth of the glacial lake, and then a ten-minute boat ride in a small yellow vessel that fits about twelve people.

The colour of the water is like a milky blue eye. The pearly effect is caused by the presence of rock flour, a substance produced as the glacier slowly moves down the mountain, collecting and grinding the rocks in its path, which then settles in the water as the ice thaws. There are several icebergs in the lake slowly melting in the sun—one shaped like a rabbit, another like a cartoon cloud. Haupapa Glacier experiences regular ice calving events, where icebergs the size of skyscrapers rush off the glacier. In the summer sun, the icebergs melt quickly. Every year, one hundred and eighty metres of ice is lost from the front of the Tasman Glacier. As recent as the 1970s, Tasman Lake didn't exist; it is the result of this ice melt and is now seven kilometres long and deeper than Lake Pukaki.

Aoraki means 'cloud piercer'. The boat guide says the mountain is obscured by mist one out of every three days and that such clear vision, like today, is good luck. The mountain is capped with white ice, or 'hanging glaciers' that are prone to falling and crashing through the valley like thunder. The closest we can get to the actual glacier is about one hundred and fifty metres because the glacier, like the icebergs, is ninety percent submerged. If we went any closer, the massive ice shelf would hit the hull of the boat.

We drive close enough to the icebergs to touch them. At first, I am hesitant to interfere, worried that the heat of my hand will exacerbate the ice melting. But I reach out anyway, place my hand flat on the icy surface, which is rough like an uncut diamond and older than I can fathom. I dip my fingertips into the cold lake, and they immediately go mauve. The temperature is about three degrees Celsius, cold to my touch. But to the glacier, this is warm, too warm, and as these giant icebergs continue to break off and thaw, the lake becomes fuller, and the warm water accelerates the melt.

After the tour, I drive the distance back to the cabin, past the burnt-down trees, and return to my daughter, who feels so warm in my arms. When she is an old woman, all of this ice will be gone.

3: Processes

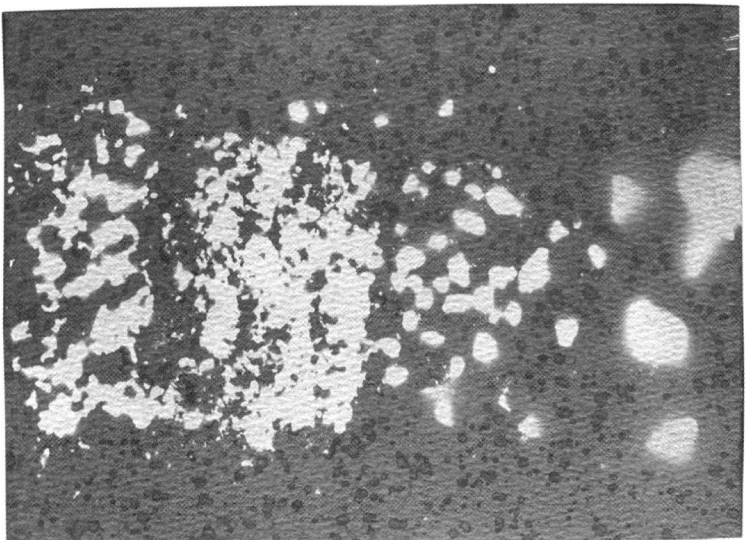

Cyanotype 3: rocks and sediment on paper, Mt Ruapehu, January 2024 (Lauren Vargo)

i. Glaciers

First comes snow, and if it's cold enough, the snow remains through the summer. Then comes new seasons and more snow. Once there is enough snow, there's enough downward pressure that it starts to compress and form ice. Once there's enough ice, there's enough mass, and that mass of ice will start to flow down the valley. *That's the technical definition of a glacier*, says Lauren, *a mass of ice that's travelling*. Glaciers gain mass in the winter and melt in the summer. Once they start melting more in the summer than they gain in the winter, there is a negative sum. Some glaciers will thin before retreating. Once they thin enough, they will retreat.

According to Lauren, the first thing you learn as a student of earth sciences is the depth of time. It is common for a teacher to address a room of eager undergraduates with a tape measure or clock. If the history of the Earth was a clock, then humans would only exist in the last few seconds. If you laid out a tape measure, humans would only exist in the last few centimetres. Cultural studies is less than a second, or a millimetre.

In her book, For Space, Doreen Massey wrote: *place is a constellation of processes rather than a thing*.[3] Glaciers are like this, a series of processes, and constantly in flux, on the move, and changing the shape of themselves, and the shape of other places. Glaciers carve up spaces like butter—*rocks make glaciers soft, glaciers leave scars on other surfaces*.

What does writing do to space? Writing about place and space memorialises it, canonises it, archives it. Essays make hard concepts soft by massaging and turning the subject over and over on itself, braiding pieces of information into something new.

Glaciers, similarly, are always flowing, gathering and preserving. Tiny bubbles of air in ice cores provide measurements of the atmosphere. Cores of ancient rock hold mud and sand that can reveal what happened here before. Glaciers are mountains that move, places that contain, and as the atmosphere warms, they become spaces that reveal—in the thawed melt of glacial ice, ash fallen from the sky indicates a fire long ago. In the Italian Alps, a 5300-year-old mummy named Ötzi surfaced in the Similaun Glacier melt. They found two fleas frozen in his clothing, the eggs of whipworm in his digestive tract, sixty-one tattoos etched with pulverised charcoal onto his skin. Maple leaves and pollen trace his death by arrow to early summer. In his new museum life, Ötzi is sprayed regularly with sterile water to prevent the loss of natural moisture. This, Lauren says, is what is so fascinating about glaciers—the information they contain. Ice, like our bodies, is solid yet impermanent. Glaciers, like our bodies—like Ötzi's body—are archival spaces.

Aotearoa's glaciers are some of the fastest-responding glaciers in the world—when the temperature warms, they are the first to melt. For example, since 2016, enough ice has melted from the Brewster Glacier to meet the drinking water needs of all New Zealanders for three years.

One of Lauren's key methods of data gathering is through visual technology and photography, making 3D models of glaciers and using visual comparison. From these images, she calculates the snowline elevation (the lowest elevation of snow on the glacier) to determine the glacier's health. The less snow there is left on a glacier at the end of summer, the more ice the glacier has lost.

In the 1970s, the National Institute of Water and Atmospheric Research (NIWA) began a photo survey, taking images of fifty of New Zealand's glaciers every year. For a long time, to study the differences year after year, Lauren says they'd hold up the photographs in front of the glacier and make a visual comparison to determine somewhere between qualitative and quantitative evaluation of change. With the major advancements in technology, instead of taking one photo, they can now take hundreds of photos of every glacier using a GPS. Unlike our phones, this GPS can tell us where we are to the centimetre. A software then creates a 3D model using these photos and GPS points. This photographic archive provides a map of loss.

Lauren shares a GIF she has made of the Brewster Glacier. It flashes stills of the ice coverage between two years. The image does the work that words cannot.

The processes leading to glacial retreat are constantly taking place, while we email, while we write on our laptops, while we speak over Zoom. Haupapa Glacier is covered in a hard rock that acts as a sunscreen for the ice, bits of blue are tiger-striped down the massive glacier. Some scientists in Switzerland, Lauren says, cover glaciers with white blankets like shrouds to prevent the sun from melting the ice, *but we can't cover every glacier in the world in blankets.*

ii. *Art making*

On her expedition to Mount Ruapehu, Lauren invited the US artist Hannah Mode to integrate an artistic practice into the science programme. Hannah's medium is cyanotypes—a form of photographic processing that uses light and water to produce blue images.

The process of making a cyanotype involves treating a surface with a mixture of ferric ammonium citrate and potassium ferricyanide, then exposing it to UV light to create an image. When exposed to UV light, the iron compounds undergo a reduction reaction, forming insoluble blue ferric ferrocyanide and the pigment also known as Prussian blue, which forms the image on the treated surface.

A cyanotype is, in a way, a co-creation with the environment: the light creates exposure, the water stops it, and the colour that is revealed—blue—has the shortest wavelength but a long cultural history (pulverised lapis lazuli allowed painters in the middle ages to create a new depth of colour to depict royalty, religion, nature).

While on the expedition, Lauren also produces cyanotypes using a variety of found material: hacking glacial ice with an axe and melting it to produce the visual effect of thaw in motion, laying wet hiking gear on the photographic paper, as well as fingertips, native grasses and flowers.

In another exercise, Hannah instructs the girls to look at a mountain or a rock, and begin a continuous free line drawing. At first, it's not clear to Lauren how this practice might be linked to science, until she realises that science is about paying attention, about keen observation. For example, when Lauren runs an exercise with the girls that involves laying a small rock on the glacier (and observing the ice underneath to determine that dark rock melts more quickly than the surrounding ice), Hannah introduces the concepts of shading, lightness and darkness.

Art making, essay writing, data analysis have this in common: they all require looking beyond the surface.

iii. *Essay writing*

There are many processes involved in the making of an essay, in the making of *this* essay: the process of connecting computers, the process of writing which is talking which is walking and watching and waiting. The process of travelling, boarding and flying through the wind, of driving four hours east to southwest in a hybrid vehicle. Of hiking, of boating, of returning. Of recruiting and exploring, of teaching and leading and drawing, of drafting, editing, and rewriting.

Carson was afraid she would turn into Emily Brontë out on those moors. Scared the cold weather would overcome her and shatter her too, hoping she might find herself reflected in the white landscape—

> A great icicle formed on the railing of my balcony
> so I drew up close to the window and tried peering through the icicle,
> hoping to trick myself into some interior vision

When we are out in these landscapes, on a glacier, beneath a mountain, on a lake, we become a part of the mechanisms involved in changing the shape and feel of a space.

Essay writing is stitching, braiding, translating, emailing, feeling. Art and essay making work associatively. Mark Tredinnick writes, 'The lyric essay does every lyric thing it can to try not to tell you what it wants to tell you'.[4] Maggie Nelson states that her work 'leans against' that of others and in so doing 'brings one into the land of wild associations'.[5] The essay is a potent landscape for these wild associations that move beyond the need to categorise the world into siloed disciplines or forms but, rather, allow the world to present itself in its full multidimensional form.

This essay leans against the work of a glaciologist and of a writer to try to not tell you something, which is not to tell you that by the year 2100 almost all of Aotearoa's glaciers will be gone.

4: Connections

When braiding an essay, or analysing data, we draw connections. Like the connections between writing and science, between the young girls on the ice, my daughter in Lake Ohau, between Wellington and the Tasman Lake that flows into the Mackenzie Basin, and these ideas that flow into each other. Like how the 2019–20 Australian bushfires dumped ash on Aotearoa's glaciers, exacerbating melting. This is one way we are connected: by our disasters, our climate, our weather. It takes three and a half hours to fly here from Australia.

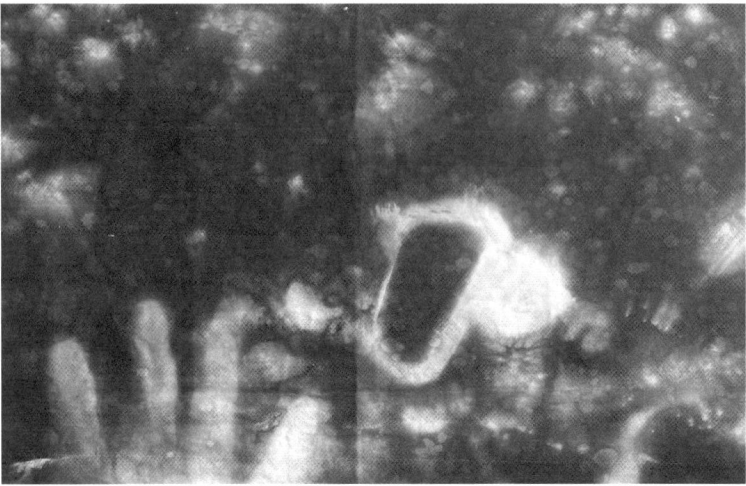

Cyanotype 4: light rain, student's fingertips and gear on fabric, Gulkana glacier, Alaska, June 2022 (Lauren Vargo)

I wonder how long it took the ash from the bushfires to float this distance across the ocean. We think about the earth as being carved up into different spaces, but one space leads to another leads to another—this is Doreen Massey's theory of place as event. What is the Earth anyway? It's a rock, or a planet, but also a series of things: books, literature, film, sounds, ice, water, bodies.

I ask Lauren what will happen to the Earth when all of the ice is gone? *It's not the mountains and plants that will be as impacted*, she says. *They will redevelop. The ice will melt, but it might come back. The Earth will become uninhabitable for humans—but when we are gone, the Earth will be fine.*

---

1   Rebecca Solnit, *Encyclopedia of Trouble and Spaciousness* (Trinity University Press, 2014).
2   Sidonie Smith and Julia Watson, *Reading Autobiography: A guide for interpreting life narratives* (University of Minnesota Press, 2010), p. 276.
3   Doreen Massey, *For Space* (London: Sage, 2005), p. 141.
4   Mark Tredinnick, 'The lyric stance', *Island Journal* 126, 2011, pp. 60–70.
5   Maggie Nelson, '"A sort of leaning against": Writing with, from and for others', *The Writer's Notebook II: Craft essays from Tin House*, by Christopher Beha (Tin House Books, 2012), p. 88.

AIRINI BEAUTRAIS & JESSICA L. WILKINSON

Re-poeming as a Practice of Making Space for Alternative Documentary Approaches

What constitutes the lifespan of a documentary poem? If documentary material is drawn into the space of a poem—which Louise Rosenblatt deemed 'an event in time' and a 'confluence of reader and text'[1]—then what might our responsibility be, as poets, to those future readers through the texts that we provide? Given our engagement with real-world 'documents', what might be our responsibility to people connected with the subject matter of our poetry? And what role might documentary poets have in handling 'difficult' material through this medium?

 We began this essay—as two poets with an interest in exploring the poem as a space for documentary practice—with a desire to compare and contrast our respective approaches to transmuting archival, site-based and other documentary research into poems, and potentially to understand what aspects of our practice (if any) might be specifically 'situated' within our respective national contexts. 'Documentary poetry' is a field in which we had both been immersed, to varying degrees, for more than a decade, through both scholarly enquiry and creative practice—we have both authored books of documentary poetry and written PhDs that explore aspects of documentary poetry and poetics through both practice and literary dissertation. We discussed how we might 'essay into' a reflection on practice together, and how we could capture a shared enthusiasm about processing research through poetry, experimenting with 'data', and writing and shaping our respective books. Yet our initial conversation quickly turned to 'trouble spots'—we have both, it seems, been reflecting on elements of our past approaches in using culturally challenging material; we have both wondered how we would do things differently if embarking on those same projects today.

This essay, then, captures a shared moment of 'essayed reckoning' as we each address a past creative endeavour in documentary poetry. In what follows, we braid our reflections on our initial intentions and discuss what we now consider to be wrongheaded approaches to aspects of our respective works. We offer new poems, too, not as a method of erasing or overwriting our previous attempts, but as possible alternative directions for sensitively navigating challenging documentary materials through poetry. This essay makes space, then, for a 're-poeming' practice to further extend the heterogeneous 'event' of the documentary poem.

Airini:
My poetry collection *Flow: Whanganui River Poems* began life as part of a creative writing PhD.[2] The creative component of the thesis was initially meant to be four or five discrete long poems. One of the long poems, which centred on the Whanganui River, became longer than anticipated; I also realised that another of the poems, dealing with deforestation in the King Country, related directly to the environmental and spiritual health of the river. I abandoned my other long poem ideas and reformulated the creative project as a single poetic sequence in three parts. Most of the material I used in my research was from secondary sources such as newspapers and historical accounts. I also drew on my own observations of the local environment, museum artefacts, and people.

I began working on my PhD in 2013. The previous year, filmmakers Christopher Pryor and Miriam Smith released the documentary *How Far is Heaven*, filmed at Hiruharama (Jerusalem) on the Whanganui River. Pryor and Smith spent a year living in the small rural community, interacting with the local people, including the three Catholic nuns who were then resident at the convent. The resultant documentary largely focused on the nuns and some of the local children but also showed vignettes of village life. It was widely praised by Pākehā critics at the time and won Best Documentary at the New Zealand Film Awards. However, I was aware of concerns some viewers had raised regarding the portrayal of Hiruharama locals—with scenes depicting gang members, underage drinking, and other negative aspects of the community, without equal emphasis on the positive. These conversations highlighted for me the importance, when making any kind of documentary, of what is included and what is left out. In documentary poetry, a lot is left out due to the constraints of the form: the segmented nature of poetry and the typically low word count. Furthermore, due to the inherently gappy nature of the poetic sequence, acts of omission and inclusion are highlighted to a greater degree. The film also made me reflect on how important our personal lens is when we are writing. *How Far is Heaven* was made through a Pākehā lens and played into familiar tropes of rural Māori that could be seen as lacking nuance and depth. It had some similarities to Taika Waititi's 2010 film *Boy* in this regard; however, Waititi (Te-Whānau-ā-Apanui) was reflecting on his own life and experience, whereas Pryor and Smith were outsiders in the community where they were filming. Part of the discomfort surrounding the film's reception by locals related to the manaakitanga that the community had shown them during their time there.

Jess:
A musician friend had told me a little about pianist and composer Percy Grainger's 'free music' experiments (inspired by sounds of the natural world and freed from metrical rhythm and individual pitch); my curiosity piqued, I began to read about Grainger's life (1882–1961) and to listen to performances of his compositions. I came to understand this strange man as not just a talented pianist but an avid folk song collector and arranger, an inventor of 'free music' machines, a rampant letter writer, a collector, an energetic hiker, a self-flagellant, and an eccentric performer. My newfound obsession led me through archives in Melbourne and White Plains, NY—the former alone held over 100,000 items. I also travelled to relevant local and international sites, pored over the many books and articles on Grainger's life and work, and listened every day to his compositions and performances. My energies were mostly focused on how I might construct a life story through this abundance of information, but also how poetry might help me to meet his unique character. This would constitute my second book of biographical poetry, and a second attempt at using poetry's unique toolkit of metaphors, rhythms, juxtapositions, gestures and lacunae to evoke 'something more' of a biographical persona from the page.

While I don't have space here to detail how I arrived at the book's specific form and structure, the poems in *Suite for Percy Grainger* became discrete entities that would take cues from certain materials.[3] For example, in a section called 'Compositions & Arrangements', the poems not only respond to those compositions named in each title (score and sound, composition notes, performance reviews) but also variously fold in other materials (biographical or historical notes at the time of composition, Grainger's correspondence or other information relating to that musical 'artefact'). The poems drew these documentary pieces together into a kind of compressed biographical collage—indeed, an expanded conception of collage became a way for me to 'deal with' the abundance of Grainger materials; it allowed me to expose and acknowledge biographical lacunae and limitation and extended an invitation to readers to participate in the 'performance' of the biography by responding to the gaps and frissons generated by juxtaposition. Quotation also enabled me to inhabit Grainger's own peculiar mode of communication (exhibited in his copious correspondence, essays and other writings).

Yet Grainger is also known for his naïve and ignorant views on race; my approach in dealing with these opinions was to proceed as per the rest of the book, to quote directly from some of his writings, enfolding his broader philosophies into poems that addressed other aspects of his life and practice. In one poem, for example, I aimed to heighten the absurdity of Grainger's 'Blue-Eyed English'—a language that he devised himself as if it were descended from Nordic roots rather than Latin-Italianate origins—through a list compilation of such words (many of them awkwardly hyphenated, and many also drawn from Māori, Danish and Norwegian but repurposed to refer to the body's sex organs or sex acts); in others, inhabiting Grainger's voice through poem was intended to summon the reader's responsiveness, their interpretive skill and ability to discern irony. In each case, I had used some typographical differences to indicate quotation (caps in one case), though I am also a little surprised that I did not make the fact of documentary quotation overly obvious, considering the sensitive and sometimes inappropriate language of the quoted material, and that I deliberately avoided a lengthy notes section at the back of the book assigning every quote to its source.

Airini:

I wrote a short introduction to *Flow*, which is titled 'Dedication.' Here, I write that:

> As the work evolved into a single entity with the river as a focus, it also became less narrative. For one thing, it is impossible to tell 'the story' of a geographical region and its people: there are many stories relating to this place and many interpretations of these stories. And, more importantly, the significance of the relationships between Whanganui iwi and the river cannot be adequately addressed by a Pākehā writer. Although six generations of my family have lived in this region on and off, and although I have a strong personal connection to the river, I felt that a unified narrative was beyond my understanding and capability, and that a fragmented approach was better suited to the way I wanted to respond to local geography and history.

In writing *Flow* I knew I was limited in my perspective and did not want to attempt an authoritative history. I wanted a mixture of voices and stories, some of which were my own, some of which were my family's, from the smallest tributaries along the river to the sea, and from ancient geological epochs through to the present. I use the lyric 'I' in many of the poems. Sometimes, 'I' is myself, the author. It is also my great grandfather, my grandfather, my father, my sister, friends of mine, living people and historical personages. I was inspired by Alice Oswald's *Dart*, but I wanted to write something longer and less linear. As it was a PhD project and my focus was on the interactions between verse form and narrative, I did a lot of formal experimentation.

I also wrote in my dedication, 'It is an attempt at something like a collage or polyphony of stories: some small, some large, some geological, some ecological, most human.' Here, I think the key phrase is 'an attempt.' I have always thought of *Flow* as a poetic experiment in form and content, an exercise book for myself, possibly even an 'interesting failure.' In some ways, I think this project, with its broad aims, could not do anything except fail. And that failure is part of what it has to offer.

Before, during and after writing *Flow* I experienced a lot of personal discomfort. Even writing about the river itself, as a body of water, seemed like a transgressive act in some ways. I see the river almost every day: it is a source of spiritual sustenance to me. However, as tauiwi, it means something different to me than it does to tangata whenua. I do not whakapapa to the river. My family and I, who have lived near it since the 19th century, have bought and sold land that was acquired under dubious circumstances.

Since *Flow* was published in 2017, some of my understandings have changed. I now feel there are a few key things I would approach differently. Firstly, I would modify my use of the lyric 'I.' I made this choice at the time of writing with the intention of contributing to the polyphonic nature of the work. Several of the poems in *Flow* are written in the first person from various perspectives. I think it is acceptable to use 'I' in the context of writing about myself or a person of a similar background; I now feel it is potentially inappropriate to use this 'I' in relation to indigenous people, particularly mythological or ancestral figures. Secondly, I would reconsider the use of material that is potentially upsetting or offensive, especially regarding events around colonisation. I don't want to erase this material, but I do think it is possible to approach it in a more culturally sensitive way. Later in this essay, I have included a rewriting of a poem, in consideration of these issues. Thirdly, I would try to engage more with iwi. At the time I was concerned about being the annoying Pākehā who takes up people's valuable time and energy seeking advice and 'blessings' for their work. But I think there is a way to engage that doesn't do this. It requires patience, but if something is worth doing, it is worth making time for.

Jess:
Last month I watched a documentary—*Swastika* (1973), directed by Philippe Mora—on YouTube. I am researching (for a new biographical poetry work) the life and artwork of his mother, Mirka Mora, a Romanian Jew who was born in Paris in 1928 and who miraculously escaped Pithiviers prison camp as a teenager a day before she was to be sent to Auschwitz. *Swastika* stitches together footage from newsreels and Nazi propaganda with excerpts of Eva Braun's colour home movies. There is no voiceover or documentary voice accompanying this collage; we move across time, through film documents, to observe the rise and fall of Nazism in Germany. Upon its release at the 1973 Cannes Film Festival, the audience broke into a riot—many interpreted the film as pro-Nazi and that it was trying to humanise Hitler.

To me, the film is like a provocative documentary poem—we are not witnessing a narrative that is simply presented to us but are called upon to sit in discomfort, to identify the irony of these juxtapositions: here we see Hitler at play with Eva, friends and children; we see footage of his political activities, of crowds won over by his powerful rhetoric; we see fit young men, proudly measured and fitted for uniforms. Mora draws us into that rip, purposely avoiding the visible suffering and horror of life at that time for Jewish people and others targeted for extermination by the Nazis. And while we feel unsettled as viewers, knowing what we know, it is only at the very end, as bulldozers push at naked bodies, that the filmmaker yanks the curtain back to amplify his message.

The crowd's response at Cannes makes me wonder about the fine line, in artworks that use collage and quotation, between an intended irony and a missed mark that opens that work to contrary, unsavoury interpretations. It raises questions about choices we make in addressing reprehensible character traits—as with Grainger's racism—in biographical poetry writing.

At a poetry event in 2019, I was asked to read from *Suite for Percy Grainger*, and I suddenly baulked at a poem I was going to read, 'The Warriors: Music to an Imaginary Ballet'. That poem incorporated a large amount of direct quoting from Grainger himself about the composition of the same title, for which he had an idealistic vision of 'primitive' warrior-types 'spirited together for an orgy of war-like dances, processions and merry-makings broken, or accompanied, by amorous interludes'. Yet as I looked at the page with its mention of 'Red Indians', I felt immediately that I could not read that poem aloud. I had not laboured over the use of these words nor sought advice. And there are other poems in the book, too, that address Grainger's racist opinions, mainly through folding his language into the poems. I wasn't blind to his racism, of course, nor to the temporal and cultural contexts within which that racism was fostered. However, this was the first time I thought that I may have been too 'playful' in my dealing with that material, relying on quotation, juxtaposition, and a future reader's careful engagement, to steer through such historical material.

Airini:
In 2021 my colleague, Lizzie de Vegt, developed a project turning a selection of poems from *Flow* into songs. With her band, she applied for funding from the Whanganui District Council Creative Communities scheme (funded by

Creative New Zealand) to record an album. Lizzie's application was initially turned down, and during the panel assessing the application, she was asked if she had consulted with iwi about the project. While this was Lizzie's project, they were my poems, and we discussed the issues that had come up.

In attempting to resolve the issues around the album, it was suggested to Lizzie one of the songs be removed. This song used lyrics from the poem 'The Sandhill.' This poem concerns part of the history of Pukenamu Queens Park in Whanganui, where a military stockade was built during the land wars. I have chosen this poem to rework for the purposes of this essay.

In 1847, five men were arrested over the killings of four members of the Gilfillan family who lived at Matarawa just out of Whanganui. A precursor to the killings had been the shooting of a Māori man by a British sailor. Four of the men were hanged at the Rutland Stockade; the fifth, aged only fourteen, was expelled from the district.

While researching *Flow* I learned about this story via a talk given by historian Paul Diamond. Diamond described how the remains of these men had been found in the 1960s during excavation works, broken up with spades, then reburied. I was shocked to learn about this, especially given that it had happened comparatively recently. In writing 'The Sandhill,' I wanted to convey the ongoing legacy of colonisation. However, I didn't consider how painful this might be for other people, nor whether I was the right person to be writing about this.

The sandhill (2017)

The sand blew from the sea mile upon mile
The black sand came in waves mile upon mile
And shaped itself into an oval hill

There was a stockade built there, and a well
A loopholed timber stockade, and a well
That watered all the rough shacks on the hill

They built a sturdy gallows on the hill
They tied four sturdy nooses on the hill
And hung four captive men till they hung still

Years later they were digging in the hill
Found four skeletons, buried in the hill
Smashed them with spades and threw them in the fill

There is a wet place, where thick grass has grown.
The old well oozes up through sand and bone.

The sandhill (2024)

The sand blew from the sea mile upon mile
The black sand came in waves mile upon mile
And shaped itself into an oval hill

There was a stockade built there, and a well
A loopholed timber stockade, and a well
That watered all the rough shacks on the hill

The loopholes looked out over a hotel
Commercial quays, and stores, and a hotel
The stockade watched the would-be city swell

And now we go and picnic on that hill
And meet for morning workouts on the hill
And drink at the colonial hotel.

There is a wet place, where thick grass has grown.
The old well oozes up through sand and stone.

I rewrote this poem to remove direct references to the execution and desecration of human remains. While keeping with the rhyming sonnet form, I have sought to address the issue of the colonial stockade in Whanganui as an acknowledgement of the violent, militarised and forceful aspects of Pākehā colonisation. I work at the foot of Pukenamu, the hill where the Rutland Stockade was built. A stone's throw away is the Rutland Arms Inn, a pub built in 1849, where I sometimes meet friends and colleagues. The 'morning workouts' described in the poem are activities I have also been involved in; the hill is also a favourite location for dog walkers. The old well is near the library where I go to borrow books. That I can go about my daily activities without the histories of this location coming to mind really brings home my own privilege. When I do think about it, it feels very strange.

I have replaced the word 'bone' with 'stone'. The story I originally wrote about is still behind this poem, but in holding space for it rather than directly describing it, I feel I am better honouring the events and the people affected by them.

Writing Flow was a useful learning process for me in terms of learning more about colonisation. I don't want to 'cancel' anything I have written; however, I think an ongoing process of reflection is always important as a writer. Having written Flow I think it is my responsibility to sit with any discomfort that I feel, to learn from it and to go forward in good faith. From here on, I feel it is my responsibility to continue to educate myself about the colonial history of Aotearoa and its ongoing repercussions; to maintain a commitment to decolonisation and to have a creative practice that contributes to this, rather than undermining it, and also to navigate how to write about landscape, nature and people in Aotearoa, across different genres, in a way that does not appropriate or misrepresent, but that also does not erase historical truths.

Jess:
In the decade since Suite for Percy Grainger was published, much has changed in the local and global literary (and socio-cultural) landscape that calls for us to be less cavalier, and more actively sensitive towards and accountable for our artistic choices. Would today's readers baulk at the repetition of some of Grainger's opinions and language in the book? While I am certain readers of

these poems would assume that repetition appealed to irony rather than literality or celebration (there being some distance in time since Grainger was alive), this reflection has sent me back to the poems and to the research notes that informed them, to find alternative tracks through to new poems that are less reliant on irony. It has also helped me to reflect on how collage and quotation—dominant techniques in much documentary poetry—might be redeployed to different effects. Further, where a narrative prose biography will most likely contextualise difficult material (and material that may 'become' more difficult as social and cultural awareness shifts and changes), this exercise has made me wonder what a poet might do in place—or as an extension—of these kinds of explanations. If readers are partially responsible for the production of a poem's 'meaning', what space are we willing to shape on the page to stimulate that process? I think again of Mora's *Swastika* as a work of collage with no intervening contextual framing and the risky provocation he extended to audiences. I am not saying Mora's approach was wrong—it is a very powerful film; rather, I am curious about the alternative interventions in tricky documentary content, beyond repetition, and what results they might yield.

Earlier in this essay I mentioned my poem 'The Warriors', which combines quotations drawn from Grainger's programme notes (the list of 'hero-types' he imagines for this 'ballet') and instructions for performers ('slow and languorous' etc) with other historical threads (Holst's 'The Planets' was composed over the same period) and characteristic Grainger expression (clumsy hyphenation, sex energy). The poem doesn't explicitly showcase or refer to the worst of Grainger's racist writing, yet it incorporates an outdated racial term from his program notes and highlights his cultural appropriation (in fact, I had not included his descriptions of body types, which shift into uncomfortable stereotypes).

Our essay reflection got me thinking about the value of repeating Grainger's terms and ideas via quotation. This approach perhaps leads to a depthless display of that historical material rather than a considered deliberation of context and consequences. Granted, the first poem captures a playful energy that drew me to Grainger in the first place, though it is perhaps the light-hearted whimsy emanating from that version of the poem that bothers me now, and I selected this poem for a 'rewrite'. In preparation, I

> ### THE WARRIORS (MUSIC TO AN IMAGINARY BALLET)
> BEGUN DEC. 1913, IN LONDON. ENDED DEC. 22, 1916, IN SAN FRANCISCO.
>
> *Our art is abstract, far from realities, is not limited to facts*
>
> Unlike Holst's upward gazing to the god-grounds Grainger's hero-types throb foot-wise to the common earth   gravity-pulled & going fast   wiring in an outpouring of the everglads & trickling good humour Wait till you hear these fierce souled phrases frolic into song   No definite program or plot though the mind pictures of swelling time and space flit into war-like action **Fast and fierce** Greek heroes, Zulus, Vikings, Amazons, Greenland women, Red Indians, Fijians, Polynesians all pride and animal spirits arm in arm and what a world entangled in the horse-haired helms & furs & beads given to the rainbow of mélange and lovemaking as if all war might shun the waste flowers **Slow and languorous** shot thru with surging onslaughts of nudism **Fast and flowing** to the bass oboe   O amorous orgies lined up at organ-point and harping vigorously **Slow** with more than one conductor **Languorous** with snatches of a third in the dark before a **Dance orgy** double-chording and commotion to the **Climax**   O again   again swelling and   **abruptly!**

returned to my copious notes about the composition and on that historical moment in Grainger's timeline; I also listened to a performance of the composition several times on Spotify. This new version of 'The Warriors' developed as a result:

> **Fast** like an engine rollicking towards momentum or newspapers reeling sharp declarations of war   furious channels of energy lead us elsewhere   Holst hooks upwards on Mars   yet Percy the pacifist   (swift as a boat set sail across the Atlantic to preserve *Australia's first composer of worth* ((and mother's health))) lands on American soil   hands feeling through earth   grope around for fierce martial rhythms and throbbing hero-types   set a jolly pace ahead of **slow and languorous** repose   certain mind-pictures set in motion these many-voiced democratic harmonies   fingers clear-sketched and writhing   out of warfare into **fast, flowing** warrior athleticism   (at least three *vigorous, strong* piano players and percussion frolicking)   Percy's **pastoral** ambition casts a hecklephone against harp harmonics and piano strings struck with mallets   peace, tranquillity?   O **languorous** listening to an offstage band   extra notes evolve in the lulls between fighting   descend   mood to mood into a **dance orgy** that reaches a **climax**   *any notes will do equally well*   just *keep on* until the orchestra splits into strands   march to a different command until   **abruptly**

Where the original poem was led by the composition itself and Grainger's own 'mind pictures', this time around I was keen to elevate the fact of WWI in the collective consciousness. It did not seem necessary to repeat his specific 'types'—his idealism of a kind of stereotypical primitive fighting (and lovemaking) spirit could be captured in other ways. It is not difficult to see that my attentions had a strong influence on the respective outcomes—the original poem juxtaposes Grainger's naive idealism with the composition's generally upbeat tone and high energy, and the second poem is situated more squarely in its time, juxtaposing the context of global war against Grainger's fear and loathing of contemporary soldiers at war, which he (anxiously?) attempts to override with his preferred imagery of primitive warrior types. I am not, in the end, convinced that this is a better poem than the original; nor am I convinced that a 'problem' is solved by avoiding certain words or terms. However, this exercise has heightened my sense of the singularity of a documentary poem and of how my particular sensitivity to documentary materials at a specific time will influence that poem's development. Beyond my concerns about handling tricky content, then, I think of the many possible poems that could be substituted here (indeed, the many versions of *Suite for Percy Grainger*) that respond to the representational problems I am confronting in any series of moments in time.

*

We opened this essay with Rosenblatt's words about a poem being an event in time that is 'realised' at the coming together of reader and text. Stephen Scobie extends this idea through the context of the documentary poem, which he says 'is never an enclosed, self-sufficient creation' but rather, an invitation to the reader 'to repeat the poet's research and engagement with the facts.'[4] In other words, while readers of documentary poems are called upon to make interpretative choices (and never to take the text at face value), readers may also be encouraged to venture beyond the poem, too, to investigate that historical terrain further. Following our brief reflections, however, we offer another possibility for nurturing the documentary poem's 'open-endedness'—that is, where frequently we might reassess our past work through academic or reflective discourse, our approach in this essay is to return to the practice of 'poeming' once more, to find new pathways through the documentary material (whether that be challenging material or otherwise). With two—or more—versions of a documentary poem sitting side by side, poetry evolves further as a rich space for ongoing documentary thinking—a space in which we can test an approach or try again, and where readers are encouraged to return to this shifting terrain of documentary engagement, to be stimulated towards new and multiple perspectives on the world.

---

1   Louise M. Rosenblatt, 'The poem as event', *College English* 26(2), 1964, p. 128.
2   Airini Beautrais, *Flow: Whanganui River Poems* (Victoria University Press, 2017).
3   Jessica L. Wilkinson, *Suite for Percy Grainger* (Vagabond Press, 2014).
4   Stephen Scobie, *Signature, Event, Context* (NeWest Press, 1993), p. 123.

AMY BROWN & JOAN FLEMING

Affidamento: The making of a shared written room

In 2019, when I was living in Madrid, I started sending Amy Brown letters about my craving for a child and my intense ambivalence about having one. She responded from the other side of motherhood. Her child, at the time, was three years old. The intensities of her duty of care as a mother, teacher and wife were of a different order to my muddled yearnings and my fears about ecological and social collapse. Amy responded with candour about the new life she found herself living and trying to make sense of.

 Our exchange has continued over the past four years and has broadened into an ongoing conversation about creative identity, compromise, sacrifice, daughterhood, domestic rage, desire, betrayal, friendship, honesty and delusion. Amy was the one to find a word for the written room we found ourselves making: affidamento. It means entrustment in Italian, and Jia Tolentino—writing about affidamento practice in the Milan Women's Bookstore Collective of the 70s—defines it as a form of space-holding where two women entrust themselves to one another, prioritising not their similarities but their differences, and affirming this difference as strength. At one point, Amy wrote, 'It's like writing a diary that replies with more than my own mind has the capacity to say.'

 This unedited excerpt is from the beginning of our affidamento.

—JF

JF [7.47pm, 29/8/2019]: It is Jordan's last night in Madrid. We eat at Wang Wangs and everyone is having bubble tea or beer and sharing the plates around, and then we walk down the street to the old man bar run by the two brothers. I have already been inside the sadness of Jordan's leaving, and now I feel light and good in the company of all these good people. Martha stands on a metal bollard in the street and smokes. She gives Jordan a smoke, and now they are nearly the same height: Jordan, who is so enormously tall and Martha, who is normally so little. Cities are so accommodating of these basic delights. I take a photo. The world should be filled with good people.

Is it my role to bring another good person into the world, to create them and raise them to be good and curious and kind? Or are these people, my friends, who I have managed to find and gather and become known to—enough? What is enough?

Later in the night, Martha and I talk about environmental collapse and motherhood. She says, what would be a better reason to fight for the world than the fact that you have a child in it? Yes, I say, but will you have the time to fight?

There are very few wild creatures in Madrid. There is a bit of wild river close to Puerta del Angel where I have seen carp and turtles. There are birds in the Retiro. There are pigeons who stop to drink the water from our swimming pool. Once in the community garden at the foot of Lavapies I saw a brown mouse in the cactus.

Sometimes the craving becomes very strong and I go and sit in one of the scrappy urban parks and I breathe for a while with my eyes closed. When I open my eyes it is like I am gulping in the blue ceiling of the sky and the shapes of the leaves.

How poor are our imaginations, that these leaf-shapes and this air and those pyramids of fruit in the greengrocers and the idea of an ocean that is living, that all these things are not enough to fight for?

I imagine when my youngest nephew is 35, the age I am now, he will ask me to remind him what a tomato plant smells like, and I will say, I can't.

JF [7.48pm, 29/8/2019]: Some mornings I wake up and the pressure of the yearning is behind my eyes and also everywhere, as if I am descending into water. Along with the pressure there is a terrible emptiness in every shape the apartment holds itself in.

I move through this heaviness and emptiness, washing my face, making tea with lemon. I knock against my grief at every turn.

I have begun to write poems about it. One I can hardly read aloud:

> She takes a picture down from the wall.
> It was always of herself
>   not anymore.

JF [7.48pm, 29/8/2019]: We would rather question physics than the economic model. This is a quote from a Professor of Energy and Climate Change at the University of Manchester. We will need three-and-three-quarter planets' worth of resources to support the existing human life on earth. Seven and a half billion people.

JF [7.48pm, 29/8/2019]: I try to think about what it is I dream about when I dream about having a child. I mean the good parts.

I imagine my child is 11 years old and has made friends with a bully, and I am listening to them and stroking their hair and somehow I say just the right thing that helps them through. I imagine being able to see this incremental growth in them, this bloom into good-personhood that would happen click by click, in all these sorts of moments. I imagine walking along the street with them and sort of wisely explaining the world to them, and seeing new lights come into their eyes.

I also imagine the chemical pleasure of their little round body and how completely I would adore their shape and their smell. I think about the specialness of their need for me and how without replacement I would be for them.

The entire experience of motherhood must be without replacement. I can fill my life with things that matter, writing and deep friendships and some kind of service. But if I choose not to have a child, I would lose this one enormous thing, the thing of motherhood. It would be a loss without replacement.

But who am I that I should have a life and not suffer loss? Last week I read this: 200 species are becoming extinct every day. Is that not an emergency? Is the earth not the more important mother?

JF [7.48pm, 29/8/2019]: Once, a friend described her darkness to me. I'm in a warehouse, she said. It's dark and has no edges and there is no one else. I'm sitting cross-legged on the concrete floor. Is it hot or cold in the warehouse? I asked.

The darkness that is with me more and more in my thirties is a fast darkness. It feels like a factory of a thousand moving parts and somehow I am all the moving parts and I am also somehow not fast enough to keep up with all the moving parts and they are rocketing ahead without me and they are saying to me: 'not enough not enough not enough'. Alternatively, they are saying: 'worthless worthless worthless'.

The factory and the voices often arrive when I am going slowly. They show up on Sundays. They show up on holidays, or when I am ill. Busy is one way to keep myself out of the factory.

I have grown up believing *busy* is an absolute value. I have grown up believing *more* is an absolute value.

Are Busy and More the parents of our economy? Our economy wants only modest growth. Three-and-half percent per year. In 24 years, that means the economy doubles. How many planets' worth of resources is that?

★

AB [12.07am, 30/8/2019]: Words at breakfast. First I read yours and they sadden me so much—I have felt a similar grief, which stopped me writing for two years when I thought we couldn't have a baby.

Milk from my son's spoon drips on my trousers. He's on my lap and we're both eating cereal. I'm reading your letter on my phone. His father sits next to us, reading an article titled '5-year outcomes of gastric band surgery in adolescents'. The radio is talking about a 'food loss bank' ('is this futuristic or a real-life plan?'). I open the blinds and ask my son what colour the sky is. 'Blue?' he says. It's very pale. 'What about down by the trees?' I ask. 'That's not the sky,' he tells me. 'That's the sunrise. Do you know why it's just above the trees?' 'No. Why?' I ask. 'Because it's warming them up.' So it is. It is 6.20am and three degrees outside.

On the drive to school, there's a new plume of smoke to the left of the Citylink—billowy as the hot air balloons floating behind it, following the Yarra. Aldous Harding's 'Treasure' fills the car with feeling. I think of the long-distance driver thought experiment, which intends to prove we can live without consciousness—we can drive kilometres on autopilot without noticing our reactions. This morning I wonder whether whole weeks can pass in this way, propelled along by a soundtrack instead of pinned in place by the news I now avoid—the voices I've come to associate with disappointment, fear and loathing.

Often, when I arrive at school, I sit in the car for ten minutes looking at my phone—emails or Instagram or interviews with Aldous Harding, for instance (this time, typing with my thumb). Steeling myself for teaching, whatever that means. 'Are we all numbers to you?' a student asked yesterday. 'No, you are people, which makes the job exhausting,' I reply. Hundreds of people glowing with anxiety and desire.

I agree that we are habituated to honour business and desire surfeit. To work and earn and consume. 'We have too much,' I think often, with the acute knowledge of my own hypocrisy. If I have too much, then I should give away the excess. I still drive to and from work, the argument being that if something should happen to my son, I need to be with him as soon as possible.

The extra time it takes to walk and catch the train is a different kind of luxury. To be alone with strangers rather than in the presence of family or students is a sort of selfishness. And yet the car is undeniably comfortable. I can be the temperature I want to be in it. I exert less energy. I fill it with music. Until I give it up, can I scorn it?

The weeks last year when I walked was when I first got pneumonia and ended up in hospital. I cannot see the illness (which returned a month ago) as simple bad luck. I must give it symbolism—of patriarchal oppression, first time around; this time, of my own frailty of character. Where is my resilience and grit? All this hypocrisy is weakening me, I think.

When I was fifteen, I did a seance with friends and the cup told me I would die at the age of 54. In 19 years' time. When my son will be 22. I don't believe in seances. But one of my friends at the table was told she would die aged 16. The following year. We laughed with worry. And then she did. This is evidence of nothing, just detail.

*

JF [6.27pm, 30/8/2019]: I was really moved by your words. I don't believe in chance or bad luck when it comes to illness. I wish I did. I believe every illness is my own fault. Too little discipline, too much dairy or sugar. Or something even more diffuse, even more generalised: weak body. Weak determination.

I would never say this to someone else, that their illness was their fault. I would never say half the things I say to myself to someone else.

To a friend, I would say: if you have a child, you'll be a beautiful mother. If you don't, you'll do a hundred other things, important things, and you'll do them beautifully. There is no right answer. There is real suffering either way.

Why is it so difficult to believe this myself, and to be light with the decision? I feel I must choose, and if I get it wrong, my life will be a sickness and it will be my fault.

It is so hard to get mothers to say the whole truth about motherhood. Rachel Zucker says that when she reads her poem 'Here Happy Is No Part of Love', about how terrifying her labour was and how happiness is a wispy emotion that has no part in motherhood, people come up to her after readings and say, you'll pay for that. Someday, he'll grow up and read that and you'll pay.

She says that when she reads it, there are often mothers in the audience, and they are often crying.

It is hard to get the whole truth out of mothers. No one ever says, 'I love my kids but I regret having them. I was a good mother, but I should never have been one.' No one says that. Maybe no one can. Yet it feels just as taboo to say, 'I yearn for a child but I'm not having one because of the health of the planet.' We will deflect the conversation anywhere else: to veganism, to giving up your car, to giving up flying, to plastic toothbrushes for god's sake. One infographic I saw phrased it this way: 'Have one less child.' If you were only ever planning on having a small family that means: Have no child.

Our friend the climate scientist just had his third child. It's difficult to understand. But then, this is the heart we are talking about, the human heart, as layered as a rose and hiding all sorts of bugs and rot in its beautiful folds. I was honestly surprised when I heard this man was a father. I was surprised when I learned he was a quite brilliant climate scientist. I don't know what I thought he was. I only ever met him at parties, late, dark, drunk, and fully deep in the nonsense. I had only ever seen him clown. One night, late and drunk at a party, he leaned over to me and Dom with a look of trouble on his face and said, 'Whatever you do, don't get married and have kids.'

As a kid, I lived completely inside my imagination. Maybe it is obvious to say that, as if every child does. But when I was walking back from the Retiro with Raquel last week, she said she is becoming, or is learning to become, more imaginative as she grows older. As a kid, she says she hardly played. Did you have an imaginary friend? I asked. No, she said.

My imaginary friend was called Becky. She was with me for years. I also had a doll called Becky. Her arms and legs and body and face were soft but she had wire inside like doll-bones and I could move her body and it would stay. I think Becky the doll was less my baby than she was my friend. I don't remember ever playing at being a mother.

But maybe I'm writing this to skew the story, to make the choice not to have a child more self-evident. Sometimes I wonder if my climate rage is just a way of being close to Dom, who doesn't want a child, not really, but will, if I do. I have hated being in this place. I feel like I am the one deciding whether to explode our lives, or not. And if we have a child, and I'm sick, unhappy, exhausted and torn all the time? What will I have blown up our lives for? One more ravenous mouth for the one percent eating up the world. One more beautiful monster, consuming their parents, pressing them dry.

I have no models of motherhood that aren't models of mothers being eaten up, eaten up completely. The closest model I have is my sister, who is so often a walking sigh, a shell, a zombie. Consumed, consuming. She made a voice-work recently, an emotional self-portrait of motherhood: layers and layers of sound and self-talk, chipper self-encouragement and rage. At its crescendo, all I could think as she played it to me through the tinny phone speakers was *turn it off turn it off*.

Is it better to have a child and to know that sea of love and to bear the exhaustion and frustration and suffocation, and the guilt of loading down the sinking ship because you so deeply wish to know that experience of kinship, or to bear the knowledge that most moments from here on in will have an empty centre, a gape where a child might have been, and the hollow virtue of knowing you've been an 'activist'?

JF [6.30pm, 30/8/2019]: When I was a kid, I used to play at burying things. Once it was a dead lizard. The only symbol for the sacred I knew was a cross, so I made one of those. The only prayers I knew were to God, so those are what I said.

In the thirty years since I was a kid, the only kin of mine who've died have been my grandparents, and they were very old and lived on a different continent and I was quite young and my parents' grief disturbed me more than my own more abstract feelings of loss. The most grief I've felt so far in my lucky life has been for lost relationships, and my never-daughter, and the earth that they tell us is dying. In the year 2000, there were 33,000 puffins.

Now, there are only 520. Scientists say the UK will be functionally infertile in thirty to forty years. There is atomised plastic now, not only in the oceans, but in the air we breathe.

I had a happy childhood, a lucky and a rich one. A blue and green one. I flew from the treehouse and when I dropped from the flying fox, I landed in the sparkling pool. My inner life was a carousel, golden light bulbs and painted horses and music and mystery and all things possible. I had all this because of my parents' professions: an obstetrician and gynaecologist mother who brought people into the world, and an exploration geologist father who dug it up.

If Dom and I had a child, they would be the child of a poet and a DJ working part-time, living on a collapsing planet. How could we ever give them that kind of life?

★

AB [11:45pm, 1/9/2019]: Over dinner with Matt on Saturday I found myself in tears (as often happens when Matt and I meet one-on-one, actually). What is it? He asked. Just too much, I said. Too much what? I wasn't sure. We'd been talking about my duty of care to a suicidal student and teacher burnout. There's a difference between a cliché and a trend, but I can't help feeling as if I'm performing predictably—a wooden caricature of a teacher in her fourth year, wondering if she'll be in the forty to fifty percent who leave the profession after five years.

At a workshop for other teachers recently, on the benefits of practising what you teach and making yourself vulnerable to student criticism by 'co-learning' rather than just instructing, a young male teacher asked whether it wouldn't be better (or enough? I can't remember his exact words) to feign vulnerability. By pretending to be writing an essay, say, in real-time alongside the students when really it was prepared earlier. That would avoid the unnecessary tension and messiness of exposing the thought process. My reaction was of immediate disagreement. False vulnerability seemed a distasteful trick. But it is one we play all the time. How is it different to any imaginative leap? Looked at in a different light, it could simply be acknowledging the limits of empathy. The teacher who writes along with her students is still less vulnerable than the students themselves, having years, practice and an aura of authority (however hard she tries to break it).

When I play with Robin, I'm usually given a role. You be Louis (Robin's friend) and I'll be Ada (Louis' little sister). Or, you be baby and I'll be mother. Robin, like most three-year-olds, it seems, adores babies and smaller children. This is enough, I tell myself as we play. He doesn't need a baby sibling so long as he can play at having one. He gets the imaginative joy of big brotherhood without the divided parental attention and inevitable stresses of a real newborn in the house. It is feigned, performed, imagined, and enough. I hope.

Growing up as an only child, my days were also green and golden and imaginative. I associate my childhood with New Zealand and often question Robin's city life. I remember playing long games in which I was a cast of many characters, sitting under the beech trees out the front of the house, personifying tennis balls (of all things)—the bald one was the baby.

There is no right or wrong, just lots of different ways of being, Nick tells me when we talk about what to do with the remaining embryo. There is no way of knowing what will be 'best', no stable definition of 'best'. Perhaps not even any choice. To even presume we can choose the best possible life seems hopelessly vain, really.

Since we've started this correspondence, everything I hear on the radio seems to regard extinction. A critically endangered sugar glider is in the way of a mine. The old white voice of the man in charge of construction says, 'If the animal is indeed still on the site [the research he commissioned found it to be absent], then we've accommodated it with corridors of habitat.' The 'corridors' will split the population and ruin its breeding season. He is clearly unmoved by the 'animals' though.

(I am so late for work now!)

★

JF [12.56am, 2/9/2019]: Thank you for sending this. It hurts my heart.

★

AB [4.05am, 2/9/2019]: I'm sorry for all the typos, and more sorry that you're hurting.

I feel like I'm skipping my turn, writing again so soon, but I wanted to add something about being consumed (and regret and pain).

I think I'm one of those consumed images of motherhood you mentioned. What I regret now isn't being eaten up, but rather the fact that I didn't know of or use this capacity for giving myself totally as a resource for a cause outside myself before having Robin. It's like state-sanctioned heroin, I remember telling Matt when he asked early on about how I was finding motherhood. If I could have abandoned myself to writing or academia in the way I did to mothering, I wonder what I could have achieved. All else seemed like vanity. That belief is what I regret. Not having more imagination.

The first sense of complete consumption came during labour—that cliché of being consumed by pain. I didn't really mind the pain eating me up until its appetite stopped seeming reasonable. When the birth started to go wrong and I knew before anyone else in the room that the pain had no point, I felt annihilated. Until then, this sense of being a natural commodity with a purpose was tolerable.

I don't know if all pain can be described in this way, but I wonder about it quite often. Is this reasonable? If so, I will tolerate it. Is this senseless or unfair? In that case, how to alleviate it? Unfortunately I suppose most pain is unfair (to the extent that fairness feels beside the point).

★

JF [4.37pm, 2/9/2019]: I remember coming to visit you in the months after you had Robin. I remember seeing your apartment in Northcote, which seemed so … so real to me, and thinking, yes, this is what 'grown up' looks like. I also remember thinking, I can't imagine how I would make this for myself.

I also remember how you said, They don't tell you. No one tells you. About the labour. No one talks about what it is really like. I don't know if you said the word 'horrendous' but horrendous is the word I remember.

I feel like I know people who give every ounce and moment of their lives over to, say, academia, or to their work. But the people I think of who do this, they are heavy, they move their bodies as if they are stones they are trapped inside of. Their faces are grey. Is academia life, can it be? What could be more a giving-over to life than giving your first and last and everything in between to the life of a child you made. But perhaps I say this to justify the limits of the energy I give to my own writing and reading, the enough that feels like enough when I put down the book or the pen. I have such spaciousness in my life. I am always just stretching out in it. I have built it that way on purpose, and I am also always teetering on the edge of an anxiety of purposelessness.

Earlier this year we took a trip to Valencia with our friend Sophia and her 8-year-old daughter Odessa. We were talking over hours about this decision, to have a kid or not have a kid, and at one point I said, maybe I won't and I'll ask my parents for my inheritance in advance and I'll use that money to just volunteer for five years for climate justice. Sophia laughed and said, either of those sound worthwhile, but just know you're not going to be thanked either way.

JF [4.49pm, 2/9/2019]: I remember thinking about the tolerable versus the intolerable when I was deciding whether to break up with Ollie. The grief and pain of breaking off our engagement felt deeply terrible. It felt like real grief. But breaking things off with Dom felt impossible, annihilating. Intolerable. So that was the choice, the horrible over the intolerable.

In that moment I had a choice, and I made it, and it was the right one, even knowing at the time that choosing Dom might well mean choosing to not have children, because of his dark feelings toward the fact of our world and his sense of ethics, that it would be wrong—for him—to bring a child into it. But also, his exhaustion after being around children for half a day. And also how fiercely he guards against being beholden or tied down in any of the usual middle-class ways. I knew all this at the time, three and a half years ago, and I chose then. Maybe I chose then, and have been grieving since?

Every time we would speak about having children, I would dissolve into tears. I couldn't have a normal conversation about it: planning, weighing, being strategic. In the months before we got married, he said, convince me. Or maybe I am misremembering. Maybe I am the one who decided I should write something, to convince him. There must be at least a part of him that wants to be convinced, because he wants me to be happy, he wants me not to harbour a resentment towards him that will rot our relationship. I wrote a poem and it was really terrible, full of cliché. 'This is not about logic. Children are the light of the world and that's not logical.' Something like that. I threw it away. I couldn't even write a poem to convince myself.

JF [4.51pm, 2/9/2019]: What you say about it being impossibly vain to think that we even have a choice—I so much want this to be true. I have fantasised and wished for an incapacity to conceive, so that it would be taken out of my hands. If I wish for something like this with such fervour, how can I in conscience try and make a baby? But ugh, I've said all this before, I'm repeating myself and I hate that. I am writing not to repeat myself but to find a new way in.

The Landfall Review

Landfall Review Online

www.landfallreview.com

Reviews posted since October 2023
(reviewer's name in brackets)

October 2023
Kind by Stephanie Johnson (Bronwyn Wylie-Gibb)
Golden Days by Caroline Barron (Gill South)
Love & Money: The writer's cut by Greg McGee (Denys Trussell)
Chevalier & Gawayn: The ballad of the dreamer by Phillip Mann (Nicholas Reid)
A Message for Nasty by Roderick Fry (Max Oettli)
A Roderick Finlayson Reader ed. Roger Hickin (David Eggleton)
Roderick Finlayson: A man from another world by Roger Hickin (David Eggleton)

November 2023
Audition by Pip Adam (Craig Cliff)
The Words for Her by Thomasin Sleigh (Elizabeth Heritage)
Kōhine by Colleen Maria Lenihan (Rachel O'Connor)
Walking with Rocks, Dreaming with Rivers: My year in the Waikato by Richard von Sturmer (Robert McLean)
Soundings: Diving for stories in the beckoning sea by Kennedy Warne (Michelle Elvy)
Travels in Eclectia by Andrew M. Bell (David Eggleton)
James K. Baxter: The selected poems ed. John Weir (David Eggleton)
From the Fringe of Heaven: Titirangi poets eds Piers Davies, Ron Riddell, Amanda Eason and Gretchen Carroll (David Eggleton)
Famdamily by The Meow Gurrrls (David Eggleton)
My Thoughts Are All Of Swimming by Rose Collins (David Eggleton)
Te Pāhikahikatanga | Incommensurability by Vaughan Rapatahana (David Eggleton)
Marcellus Wallace's Dirty Laundry by David Beach (David Eggleton)

December 2023
Robert Lord Diaries eds Chris Brickell, Vanessa Manhire and Nonnita Rees (Murray Edmond)
Pet by Catherine Chidgey (Kay McKenzie Cooke)
We Need to Talk about Norman: New Zealand's lost leader by Denis Welch (Helen Watson White)
Āria by Jessica Hinerangi (Siobhan Harvey)
As the trees have grown by Stephanie de Montalk (Siobhan Harvey)

Middle Youth by Morgan Bach (Siobhan Harvey)
Garments of the Dead: Old and new work by Koenraad Kuiper (Piet Nieuwland)
Saga by Hannah Mettner (Piet Nieuwland)
Liveability by Claire Orchard (Piet Nieuwland)
Artists in Antarctica ed. Patrick Shepherd (David Eggleton)
Ki Mua, Ki Muri: 25 years of Toioho ki Āpiti eds Cassandra Barnett and Kura Te Waru-Rewiri (David Eggleton)

February 2024
Hiwa: Contemporary Māori short stories eds Paula Morris and Darryn Joseph (Vaughan Rapatahana)
The Seasonwife by Saige England (Tina Shaw)
Mila and the Bone Man by Lauren Roche (Michael O'Leary)
Jenny McLeod: A life in music by Norman Meehan (Sally Blundell)
Shadow Worlds: A history of the occult and esoteric in New Zealand by Andrew Paul Wood (Jack Ross)
Selling Britishness: Commodity culture, the Dominions and Empire by Felicity Barnes (David Eggleton)
Sure to Rise: The Edmonds story by Peter Alsop, Kate Parsonson and Richard Wolfe (David Eggleton)

March 2024
Dream Girl by Joy Holley (Jenny Powell)
Signs of Life by Amy Head (Jenny Powell)
Our First Foreign War: The impact of the South African War 1899–1902 on New Zealand by Nigel Robson (Nicholas Reid)
I Don't Believe in Murder: Standing up for peace in World War 1 Canterbury by Margaret Lovell-Smith (Nicholas Reid)
Defending Trinity College Dublin, Easter 1916: Anzacs and the Rising by Rory Sweetman (Nicholas Reid)
Who Disturbs the Kūkupa by Kayleen Hazlehurst (Nicholas Reid)
Urgent Moments: Art and social change: The Letting Space projects 2010–2020 eds Mark Amery, Amber Clausner and Sophie Jerram (Andrew Paul Wood)
Fierce Hope: Youth activism in Aotearoa by Karen Nairn, Judith Sligo, Carisa R. Snowden, Kyle R. Matthews and Joanna Kidman (Andrew Paul Wood)
Past the Tower, Under the Tree: Twelve stories of learning in community eds Balamohan Shingade and Erena Shingade (Andrew Paul Wood)
Ngā Kupu Wero ed. Witi Ihimaera (Jeffrey Paparoa Holman)
End Times by Rebecca Priestley (Wendy Parkins)
Don Binney: Flight path by Gregory O'Brien (David Eggleton)

I Am Painting the One Picture All the Time

Ian Wedde

Gordon Walters by Francis Pound (Auckland University Press, 2023), 464pp, $89.99

I'll start with some short samples of Francis Pound's text selected from many options in this immense book. They allow me to identify a few of its key qualities. Just over halfway through, in Chapter Eleven, 'Development of the Koru Series', a heading most readers, myself included, may assume announces the book's core moment, we read this under one of the chapter's subheadings, 'Sudden spasms and the reserve':

> However, there is an irregularity amidst all this regularity that cries out to be mentioned. In a sudden spasm, the top register's lowest red ochre bar turns down at right angles to itself, as if bent back in collision with the frame, defying the by now well-established law of the horizontality of the koru bars. A similar paroxysm seizes the fourth stripe down of 'Koru Study: White/Grey/Yellow/Black' (1966/73), again disrupting the smooth, continuous, expected flow of the bars, but this time jerking the bar's end up rather than down.

A couple of pages earlier, in a chapter subsection titled 'Brutality and the return to colour', I encounter the phrase 'the sheer hardness and vehemence of what remains', and a little further on, in Pound's discussion of the influence on Walters of American minimalists, especially Frank Stella, during the 1950s and early 60s, there's the following: 'Walters was surely encouraged to stick with his pitiless stringency …' And, a not entirely fortuitous coincidence, in one of the great many lengthy marginal notes that enrich this book's discursive layers, a distinctly sarcastic reference to the likelihood that Colin McCahon was influenced by Walters' 'pitiless stringency': '… though this is something no one will ever admit, since everything that McCahon does must always be entirely unprecedented.'

So: we're informed by implication that everything Walters did may have developed to greater or lesser extents from precedents that encouraged him in his 'pitiless stringency' and 'sheer hardness and vehemence', resulting for example in a 'sudden spasm' and a 'paroxysm … jerking the bar's end up'. This is language that dramatises the author's experience of dynamic and even sensational artworks that many, myself included, have read as cool and restrained—minimal both in their subtle impacts and in terms of their art-historical moment as associated for example with what 'has been called the first minimalist show: Black, White and Grey, at the Wadsworth Atheneum, Hartford, Connecticut, in 1964'.

Pound's language is immensely stylish, surprising, and infectiously eloquent. It's a great pleasure to read in itself, but also because what at first seemed hyperbolic ('cries out') startled me into a fresh way of looking at Walters' work. Here, then, are two of the book's key qualities: its stylish language and that language's provocation of a revitalised response to the dynamism of the work being described.

A third quality is found in the reference to McCahon (45 out of 55 substantial marginal notes in this chapter, 'Development of the Koru Series') which, as well as representing the highly unusual quantity and length of such notes throughout the book as a whole—a demanding and even eccentric book-within-a-book component—points to one of its major themes and accomplishments. This is the scrupulously and exhaustively documented in-depth scholarly account of Walters' search for and explorations of international models for his practice outside the claustrophobic confines of the New Zealand art scene from the time of his early experiments in the 1940s with what the Auckland City Art Gallery director Peter Tomory called the 'cliché' in which 'burnt forests and tortured tree roots writhed about the hills'. As Pound writes in Chapter One, 'Beginnings', '[H]e was demanding more of himself than a small, provincial culture demanded: setting himself an inward standard of excellence, based on distant European models.'

A key encounter within this thematic was with the Dutch/East Indian émigré Theo Schoon, who introduced Walters not only to aspects of contemporary European art, but also to what should be learned from the art and thought of non-European cultures; and that one could learn too from 'such groups as children, the mad, and the "primitive".' Walters' relationship with Schoon was not unproblematic, but the consequences of Schoon introducing him to Māori rock art, for example, would be long lasting and profound. The influence of Schoon's own artwork (which Pound describes as 'really rather dreadful') was unimportant; Pound quotes Walters as saying, 'I never actually liked his painting very much. In fact, I didn't like it at all.' Pound suggests that the young Walters 'prefers to immerse himself in reading rather than look at Schoon's paintings'. And the book goes on to document in great detail the quantity and persistence of Walters' lifelong research through art books and catalogues, as well as (eventually) through travel to Britain and Europe.

The outbreak of war in 1939 delayed Walters' planned journey to Europe. But in 1950, as Pound dramatises the moment in Chapter Four, 'The Journey to Europe: London and Paris', 'He was thrust into a state of impassioned receptivity, in which he was enabled to absorb sufficient to last him for the rest of his life.' A characteristic Poundian marginal note both qualifies and expands on this drama: Pound records that he heard Walters identify two pre-Europe moments as critical to his development, the first being his study of academic drawing under Schoon, the second the wartime discussions of modernism among 'the European refugees at the Ministry of Supply' (where Walters worked during the war). In this chapter we read both an account of the hostility to abstract art in New Zealand, for example where A.R.D. Fairburn wrote of 'the falseness of all abstract art' and 'the death-corpse-stinking falseness and utter dishonesty of Picasso'; and a scrupulously researched and documented record of what Walters saw and heard—a lot!—during his travel.

Critically, as well as benchmark encounters with the actual rather than reproduced work of Mondrian and other European abstract artists, Walters also saw 'examples of tribal art sensitively displayed in galleries as works of art'. And, 'I understood too how much of the vitality of twentieth-century European art came from the discovery by artists of this material.' And, '[It] was only by coming to terms with my being a New Zealander that I could go on to paint', Walters said in a lecture at the Auckland Art Gallery in 1983.

He was 31 when he went to England and Europe and, as Pound emphasises in the Chapter Four subsection 'Walters' Pre-journey Reputation', had already honed an accomplished figurative style and was on the edge of a successful career as an artist. But as a consequence of seeing the abstract work of artists including Mondrian, and the presentation of 'primitive' art in museums, he built 'a conception of his art as, in essence, a constructive operation with elementary, non-mimetic forms'. Here Pound quotes the great American art historian Meyer Schapiro, who was in fact writing about the 'astonishing conversion' of Mondrian, 'an accomplished painter of nature at the age of forty'.

This is one of the most illuminating revelations in Pound's book, an expansion of the third quality noted earlier, the scrupulously documented in-depth scholarly account of Walters' search for and explorations of international models. What's striking about the companioning with Mondrian, however, is a fundamental difference in Walters' situation: the intimate proximity in his own country of Māori art, as first pointed out to him by Theo Schoon but reinforced by his encounters with tribal art in the museums of Europe.

His 'conversion' when confronted with works by Mondrian, and several others including (up to a point) the geometricism of Auguste Herbin at the Denise René gallery in Paris, was complete enough, given the hostility towards 'abstract' painting in New Zealand in the 1950s, to lock him out of a local art world in which, as Pound notes acidly of artists including Toss Woollaston, the nineteenth-century example of Paul Cézanne was the innovative limit. And even Cézanne, Pound notes, was too much for 'the New Zealand Academy and the arts society painters, those middle-aged amateurs for whom Cézanne seemed utterly beyond the pale'. Let alone the work of the 1950s Americans that Walters looked at, including Ellsworth Kelly.

Among the abstract works to which Walters began to develop approaches following his return to New Zealand, Pound includes a gouache on paper, *Study for Grey/Pink* (1955), a fully abstract, geometric work of rectangles with a central pinkish square. Other works of gouache on paper using rectangles include *Untitled [Four Vertical Men (Red, Green, Yellow, Blue)]* (1955)—the square-bracketed titles are Pound's intervention, fully accounted for in his early methodological notes. The hint of figuration these works introduce is consistent with other works yet to be encountered, and also with Walters' omissions of descriptive titles. No such intervention was found necessary in the case of Fig. 90 on page 101, which is the first full-page koru-based work illustrated in the book, *Untitled No. 4* (1956, ink on paper, 278 x 218mm). It consists of what will become the black/white, figure/ground ambiguity composition of subsequent koru-based works, in this early surviving example incorporating a koru shape as yet unrefined and retaining an upcurved bulb and sinuous stem.

It's at this point in his career that Walters' rigorous pursuit of a methodology for an abstract art that would eventually become capable of incorporating the geometric potential of the koru resulted in his exclusion from the art world for almost 20 years. It also resulted in his destruction of almost all the gouache (and gouache and ink) on paper works of the 1950s—years during which he was working full time with little to spare for his art, little or no time to develop the gouaches into paintings, and no gallerists or collectors willing to support his practice.

Then came a breakthrough. Pound begins Chapter Twelve, 'Te Whiti', with a marvellous quote from Walters from 1966 …

> I am painting the one picture all the time … It doesn't matter what the subject matter is, I am trying to perfect the one thing I was meant to do. To perfect it to my satisfaction. It is an unattainable thing, but you have it there right in front of you, all the time.

Pound goes on to ask, rhetorically, '[W]hy did he choose to abandon seventeen years of silence by letting a solitary and undefended single work out into so unmistakably hostile a world?' The occasion was the exhibition Abstract Paintings by Forty New Zealand Artists in early March 1966, preceded by the Hay's Prize competition exhibition. The painting was entered in the Hay's Prize with the title *Painting 1965* and in the Abstract Paintings exhibition as *Te Whiti*—a kind of progressive coming out that also marked the first major sale of a painting by Walters, significantly a koru painting. The exhibition organiser, funder and curator was Baron Ralph von Kohorn, a German-born American businessman living in Wellington and the first purchaser of *Te Whiti*. With a hint of timely melodrama, Pound notes of this moment that '"Te Whiti" comes as a rising up from a dark reserve. Its parts seem incomparably placed and held.'

His book goes on in the following chapter to document Walters' solo exhibition at Kees Hos' New Vision Gallery in Auckland in March 1966, from which fewer than half of the 12 paintings survive, but which marked his entry into the active art world; and moves on through four further chapters to cover the varieties of ways in which Walters continued to explore 'the one painting'. Pound's account of the rigour of these explorations, especially in the 1980s and 1990s 'Transparency' paintings (Chapter Sixteen), reads like a reaching back through the impulses and unflinching denials of the preceding 40 years, a narrative that has required a complementary and appropriately admiring homage in Pound's scrupulous account. The late Untitled [Transparency with Light] (1994) and Untitled [Transparency with Shadow] (1995) are, like the majority of Walters' works, not based on the koru but consist of twin rectangles, of which the left one is overlaid on its left side by a delicately diaphanous top-to-bottom stripe that modulates the colour of the rectangle beneath.

To complement Pound's salute to the artist's vitality ('sheer hardness and vehemence') I want to add this viewer's encounter with works of great refinement and subtlety that have a stillness that reflects an arrival or accomplishment, reaching back to works begun in the mid-1950s, abandoned in the 60s when the koru works predominated, and retaining the trace of Walters' encounters with the overlay works of Josef Albers. As Pound notes,

'The Transparencies became a major part of Walters' painting of the '80s and '90s, issuing in an unbroken procession ended only by the artist's death.'

The fourth key quality revealed in the text is the book's debt to its several editors; and to the lucid overview of one in particular, Leonard Bell, who has contributed excellent Fore- and Afterwords, and also managed Pound's unabashed and generous use of and homages to the scholarly work of Michael Dunn.

This is without doubt one of the most important art books written in New Zealand, not just about the artist of its title, but also the complex international art history of which Gordon Walters has been a part. Dr Francis Newport Pound, who died in October 2017, made the turning of these pages into an experience of innovative, scrupulous and immensely detailed scholarship, regularly laced with dry humour.

A History of the Nation's Reading
David Herkt

The Book Collector: Reading and living with literature by Tony Eyre (Mary Egan Publishing, 2023), 276pp, $45

In Ray Bradbury's novel *Fahrenheit 451*, all books are banned by the state because they lead to its citizens becoming unhappy by discovering competing ideas. In François Truffaut's 1966 film adaptation of the book, a glossy red, low-slung, electric-powered fire truck, with a salamander hood ornament, speeds to suburban homes where its firefighters locate concealed libraries and torch them with the aid of flame-throwers. Sometimes book owners choose to be immolated with their small collections.

As the books ignite, crumple and turn to ash, Truffaut's camera lingers on the covers: *Othello*, *Don Quixote*, *Lolita*, *The Catcher in the Rye*, *Zazie dans le Métro*, Sade's *Justine*, *Alice's Adventures in Wonderland*, *Madame Bovary*. It is a prescient film. The plot focuses on one fireman, Montag, reading a proscribed book out of curiosity, only to discover a fascination for literature.

Somewhat surprisingly, the attitudes of the society depicted in the movie are beginning to be on open display in the contemporary world, often in places one would least expect, including its public libraries, through the actions of some librarians. As if in opposition, Tony Eyre's *The Book Collector: Reading and living with literature* is a record of the richness of one man's life seen through the perspective of his love for literature and the collecting of its emblematic artefact, the book. It is an autobiography, a guide, a travelogue and a wide account of New Zealand publications. It is also a useful overview of the contemporary market for used and first editions, not to mention vintage popular publications and other printed ephemera.

The dust-jacket image of the first edition of Janet Frame's *Owl's Do Cry*, published by Pegasus Press in 1957, is, as Eyre mentions, arguably the most evocative of all New Zealand book covers. It reflects a particular society and era in all its local specificity. It was designed by Dennis Beytagh, a Shanghai-born illustrator who trained at London's Central School of Arts and Crafts and worked in British publishing before moving to New Zealand in 1955. He saw a newer nation through fresh but expert eyes.

Eyre writes:

> The flat images of an eerie night-time streetscape, as viewed from an upstairs hotel room, looks down on the illuminated Kiwi Milk Bar with a silhouetted motorbike rider and his pillion passenger preparing their departure ... Other buildings in the main street, like the Bank of New Zealand, barely emerge from the shadows but the Grand picture theatre (with its overhead veranda, spelling out in light bulbs its feature movie, *Owls Do Cry*) casts out a warm glow, as a comfort perhaps to a departing guest, emerging into the lamplight.'

In an era of the transient and the evanescent, when everything flickers into attention for a bare instant, the solidity of this evocation of a lost time is haunting. While the design of contemporary dust-jackets is dominated by the condensed brevity of the graphic swish and glossy colours of commercial demand, Eyre directs his reader towards a different world, one in which he is staking a claim to be a gentle but significant explorer.

While *The Book Collector* is ostensibly the record of a man and his life through the mirror of the books he enjoys and collects, and which educated him, it is far more than that. It is also a history of a nation's reading.

The extent to which New Zealand has been culturally created by bibliophiles can easily be seen in the origin of its libraries. In 1887 Auckland Public Library benefited from Sir George Grey's gift of his own 15,000-volume collection, which included a first folio Shakespeare, as well as various medieval manuscripts, many books and documents in Māori, and even the original words and music to 'God Defend New Zealand'. In Wellington, Alexander Turnbull's vast library came into national ownership upon his death in 1918. That library now holds a world-class collection of Milton, and many early books published in or about New Zealand and the Pacific. Dr Thomas Hocken created the nucleus of the Hocken Collections in Dunedin. He located the only surviving signed copy of the Treaty of Waitangi in a pile of discarded and damaged papers in a government basement in 1903. Along with these libraries of national significance there are those of smaller collectors, whose books may only have been assembled for the lifetime of their owners. Some had broad interests, others a more focused vision.

Born in 1953, Tony Eyre spent his first years in Avondale. He learned to read in a Catholic primary school using Janet and John readers. Soon there would be British comics—*Lion*, *Tiger* and *Marvel*, with the more compact *Commando*. The needs of life, education, his career as a chartered accountant, marriage and children somewhat buried him for a number of years before a 'hankering to make up for lost time' led to his discovery of William Faulkner, Flannery O'Connor, Muriel Spark, Daphne du Maurier and Jack Kerouac.

Eyre is a New Zealander of a certain generation. He was committed to Corso, the Council of Organisations for Relief Service Overseas, whose co-convenors were the Red Cross, the National Council of Churches, and the Quakers. He organised Trade Aid sales for Corso from the back of a VW Combi and volunteered for the Stella Maris Seafarers' Centre, an organisation that provided welcoming hospitality to visiting sailors. It was a world in which New Zealand was a caring place.

He describes the Mechanics' Institutes, founded in 1800 to give 'working men' educational opportunities. The Dunedin branch (of which Eyre is currently president) is still manifested through its well-used lending library, the Athenaeum, which might not trumpet its existence in the Octagon but more than fulfils a role in the city's intellectual and cultural life.

Eyre also developed a passionate interest in New Zealand writers, with an especial admiration for the works of Invercargill-born Dan Davin, eventually a publisher at Oxford University Press, the author of numerous short stories and novels, as well as Crete, the best of the official war histories. Eyre prizes Robin Hyde, too, author of The Godwits Fly and Passport to Hell. He excels in providing two- or three-page summaries of a writer's life, their works, and—most importantly—their meaning for him.

The Book Collector also functions as a study of the present-day New Zealand second-hand book trade and could profitably be used as a guide for a visiting bibliophile. Eyre describes locations, layouts, contents and the shops' owners in a lively but considerate prose. A single book is often selected from the stock and highlighted to effect.

In Rotorua's Atlantis Books, for instance, Eyre found a first edition Sylvia Ashton-Warner in a scarce American printing, as well as a long-sought book by a friend of Dan Davin, Winifred McQuillan, who wrote schoolgirl novels under the pseudonym Clare Mallory. In checking behind the first bank of a shelf of unwanted children's classics, he discovered a 1947 copy of Mallory's Merry Again, with the green gym-smocked schoolgirl beaming on the pristine cover.

Many of the byways of second-hand book purchase are explored. There are the great all-day sales of service clubs such as Rotary, and Dunedin's annual 24-hour Regent Theatre book sale with its prison-like shuffle of packed buyers around the constantly replenished trestle tables. Then there are the hushed and polished tones of Anah Dunsheath's antiquarian shop in Auckland's High Street, with its stock of leather-backed sets. Eyre gives accounts of bookshops in Australia, London, Ireland and Singapore. There is a visit to China. He discourses just as easily upon an edition of Quotations from Chairman Mao, with political alterations to the text in the wake of Lin Biao's death, as he does on Dan Davin's hard-to-find 1945 Cliffs of Fall, with a paper cover 'folded concertina-like at the back'.

It would be an obtuse reader who did not delight in Eyre's account of Elsie Summers, whose 50-odd Mills and Boon novels, most with New Zealand settings, collectively sold over 20 million copies between 1957 and 1997. Eyre's definition of New Zealand literature is broad, and he is living proof that knowledge is a useful thing as he unearths valuable volumes in unlikely places.

Offering first-hand reportage, Eyre writes of one Auckland shop owner: 'Heather Northey is always sitting in her corner by the window, her presence a reassuring constant, given the challenges facing any small bookseller to keep their doors open.' However, by the time Eyre's book was published, the 99-year-old-owner of Northey's shop had died. The subsequent dramatic rent increase for the premises made Dominion Books financially unviable for the first time in 37 years.

In the 1970s New Zealand libraries saw microfilm as heralding the end of the paper book. The National Library began microfilming its collection of newspapers and magazines, often discarding the originals. There were skip-bins in the Wellington library loading docks overflowing with disassembled volumes.

But, as the libraries soon discovered, the book was here to stay, and microfilm (and microfiche) came with their own problems of preservation and access. Libraries are now faced with maintenance of 50-year-old machines with limited usefulness. Later, ebooks were also thought to be the replacement for paper books, but will ebooks endure beyond the next iteration? Are they even read in the same way as their paper precursors? Do they actually replace them? And if the medium is indeed the message, as the Canadian technological theorist Marshall McLuhan has suggested, how do their contents change?

Bradbury's *Fahrenheit 451* concludes when people begin to fight against the proscription and burning of physical books in the only way they can—by returning to a Homeric oral tradition. Small gatherings of social rebels, who have each chosen to memorise one or two books in the face of global collapse, recite them around rural campfires outside the dangerous cities.

Eyre's *The Book Collector* has a vital underpinning philosophy, as heartening as that of the literary outlaws of *Fahrenheit 451*. It is a companionable book with a large message.

The Place of the Heart
Simone Oettli

Tangi: The 50th anniversary edition by Witi Ihimaera (Penguin, 2023), 256pp, $30

In his 2023 NZSA Janet Frame Memorial Lecture, Witi Ihimaera told his audience that he began his writing career by imitating Janet Frame's first collection of short stories, *The Lagoon*. The result, his book *Pounamu Pounamu*, was published in 1972. The final story in the collection was called 'Tangi'. What he failed to imitate, until he published his last version of *Tangi* in 2023, was Frame's habit of not punctuating dialogue. He tried back then, but the lack of punctuation was met with opposition from his publisher.

Ihimaera tells us that 'Tangi' was originally written as an independent short story in 1969 and appeared in *Contemporary Māori Writing* in 1970. Keeping the same title, he developed the short story into his first novel while he was in England with his wife, Jane Cleghorn, and it was published in 1973. The dedication reads: TO MY FATHER. In 2005 an expanded version was published as *The Rope of Man*.

Last year, half a century after the first novel, Ihimaera published another expanded variation, while going back to the original title, *Tangi*. Are we to assume this will be his last attempt? The urge to rewrite has become something of a habit (*Pounamu Pounamu* was revised and republished in 2022). But whereas the first *Tangi* was written in the present tense, *Tangi II*, as I will call this iteration, is written in the past tense, suggesting that Ihimaera sees this version as the final word.

The basic story could, in some ways, be termed autobiographical. There is a strong fictive element but nonetheless, in their essence, the characters and places in the book are not fictional. As in the first novel, the main theme of *Tangi II* is set out at the beginning and repeated at the end of the book. It derives from the Māori creation myth: 'My mother was the Earth. My father was the Sky. They were Ranginui and Papatūānuku.'

However, the 1973 version of *Tangi* was not about the protagonist's parents but, as the title indicates, about a tangihanga or funeral. The novel followed his attempt to come to terms with the unexpected death of his father. In this respect the recent novel is more accurate.

Ihimaera's mother, and then his father, died in 2010. Both books are dedicated to Tom; that is, as the author elaborates in *Tangi II*, to Te Haa O Rūhia (Czar of all the Russias), known as Tom Smiler, and in the story he is identified with Ranginui: 'My father was like Ranginui. He held dominion over night and day. He was both sun and moon, keeping constant watch over his children. Every day he rose to keep Papatūānuku warm.'

Both books are full of aroha. They were written in the first person, from the perspective of Tama. Which could raise the question of how Ihimaera felt about his own father. Why did he seemingly use a book to kill him off prematurely? In reply to this, Ihimaera reminds us that the book is 'an account of death, but also an affirmation of life'. As he asserts in the introduction to *Tangi II*, both versions describe 'simply and sincerely the Māori values placed on life; and on aroha, love and sympathy for each other'. They were 'written to ensure that such a life, and the values of that life, will never be lost'.

It is relevant here to remember that the first novel was written nearly 30 years after the beginning of the Māori urbanisation movement, when for many Māori those values were fast disappearing. Ihimaera himself was part of the exodus. In fact one of the issues raised by *Tangi* is the consequences of leaving a country marae for the city.

Both novels show Tama as very fond of his father, and the portrait Ihimaera has drawn of Tom captures his essence in a remarkable way. He was an intelligent and friendly man with a good sense of humour, a great sportsman and a hard worker. I have an image of him way up high, conscientiously painting the tāhuhu (ridge beam) of Rongopai, the meeting house in Waituhi, with his daughter, Polly. They were both fearless. Tama's father is named Rongo, presumably after the god in Māori mythology who cultivates kūmara and is a protector of crops.

Although his mother plays a minimal part in the first *Tangi*, Tama in *Tangi II* has a strong bond with Huia, who is symbolised by Papatūānuku. In neither book does his mother die, yet in real life the tangi of Ihimaera's mother took place nine months before his father's. We are dealing here with fiction, as the author himself points out. And yet the central characters—Tama, Tama's three sisters, and Rongo and Huia—bear a strong resemblance to the personalities of Witi Ihimaera, his siblings and his parents, Tom and Julia.

It is not until the end that we realise that Tama is mistaken when he answers his own question: 'What is worse: the loss of a mother, or the passing of a father?'

> I suspect that if, in fact, Mum had been the one to die, I would probably have returned to Wellington to resume my job. Dad would have grieved over Mum, but got back to running the farm. My sisters would have looked after him. Simple. Easy as. When your mother is the surviving parent, however, and you are the eldest son, it's different.

His father is not as strong as Tama believes. Before he dies, Rongo asks Tama to help with the lambing season. Tama refuses. He has a job in Wellington and cannot take the time off. When Rongo dies before the end of lambing, Tama deeply regrets his decision. 'You should have asked me one more time, Dad,' becomes a refrain throughout the book. Not, as his mother points out, that it would have made any difference. As she tells Tama: 'None of us could have stopped this from happening.'

The relationship between Tama and

his father, as well as Tama's feelings for Rongopai, are defined in terms of the heart: 'for me, Rongopai was like my father. Home. The place of the heart.' This establishes the centrality of the meeting house, as well as the emotional hold it has over the iwi. Rongopai is the centre of *Tangi II*; it is the sacred meeting house where Rongo lies in state for three days to allow whānau to farewell him.

Rongo prepares Tama for death: 'My father helped me to imagine the dead travelling astrally across the mountains, shores, lakes and plains of Aotearoa to arrive one by one at the northernmost beach.' This is Piwhane, or Spirits Bay, from where Māori believe the spirits of the departed leave for the afterlife. But before he travels north, the spirit of Rongo appears to Tama twice. The first time he reminds his son that it is lambing time and tells Tama he knows what to do. The second time, when he appears sitting next to Tama on the flight to Gisborne and his own funeral, he is not well received. Tama says: 'Go and pick on someone else, Dad. Let me grieve by myself.'

Tama's image of his mother turns out to be inaccurate as well. Huia is portrayed as having powerful, close relationships with both Tama and Rongo. She is a strong and independent woman, courageous and wise as well as stubborn and disobedient. When, on a cold, snowy morning during lambing, Rongo goes out to see to the ewes, and his horse later returns without its rider, Huia knows instinctively that her husband is dead. She goes out to look for him and finds him lying on the ground, 'spangled in snow crystals'.

'Couldn't you have waited, Darling, to say goodbye to me?' she asks as she hoists him onto his horse to bring him home. Once the funeral is over, Huia proves more capable and competent than Tama had expected. Rongo had treated her as an equal and she was used to doing a man's job in all kinds of weather. When Tama offers to come home, she is adamant that she can cope with the farm on her own. She points out that she has her three daughters and their husbands to rely on, if needed.

Essentially *Tangi II* is a book about parenthood. Unlike in the first *Tangi*, the parents are here given equal weight. Time after time, Tama recalls events he experienced involving one or other of them. The whole story is held together and punctuated by references to his journey to and from the tangi in Waituhi. This gives the novel a time-frame, and also allows the story to be told in the characteristic shape of a spiral, with shifting perspectives that range from the factual to the emotive. And at long last *Tangi* has no punctuation to indicate dialogue.

The story has been told four times. The short stories in *Contemporary Māori Writing* and *Pounamu Pounamu* gave us the bare bones. In his first novel, Ihimaera dwelled on Tama's reaction to his father's death and outlined his experience at Rongo's tangi. *The Rope of Man* introduced the perspective of

Tama's mother, Huia, which was reinforced in *Tangi II*. As readers we get the impression that in the latest *Tangi* everything has been completed; all the elements have finally been accounted for and resolved.

Hope Waved to Her Almost Beyond her Vision

Bronwyn Wylie-Gibb

Bird Life by Anna Smaill (Te Herenga Waka University Press, 2023), 296pp, $38

Anna Smaill's latest novel, *Bird Life*, begins with a vividly atmospheric description of a park in contemporary Tokyo. The park is idyllic: it is blossom time, pollen gilds the air, a whimsical fountain spouts intermittently as people stroll, trap pigeons (what? why?) and eat lunches of eel-and-rice.

A Japanese woman walks in the park, 'a picture of middle-class, middle-aged femininity', elegant with her very proper clothes and Louis Vuitton bag. Her slight disarray—a single shoe, torn stockings—is not immediately obvious, she is so dignified. On a square of grass she sees a young foreign woman, sprawled, apparently motionless but almost vibrating with anguish. The woman walks closer—the pollen drifts, the fountain suddenly spurts, startling people and birds, and then we leave this moment for the next 100 pages.

This is a wonderful way to put us inside the world of the book: we are in Japan with Dinah, a New Zealander teaching English to undergraduate engineering and science students. She has just arrived. Everything she sees is new, slightly odd and strange. But Dinah is slightly odd and strange herself; she is muted, rather than excited about this adventure in a new land. She moves through her days in a sort of haze: going to and from the university, teaching, buying just enough food and drink to survive on—and avoiding her apartment, sleeping instead on a bench in the small park next to her building. She is so isolated, so sad.

The Japanese teachers of English have their own room and do not interact with the non-Japanese teachers. Dinah desperately misses her late twin Michael; her memories of him, of their shared life seem much more real than the Japan she is drifting through. Michael was an unusual child who behaved in ways that made the other children stand back and that bothered the adults. He became a brilliant classical pianist yet he had serious mental health issues. He was the originator of a game the twins played from early childhood called It's Only Us Now, where, gripping each other's hands, they ventured out into a world imagined as suddenly de-peopled. They stole food, made themselves a safe nest in the garden. On her bench in a park in Japan, a bereft Dinah yearns for Michael.

Yasuko is one of the Japanese teachers of English. She dresses smartly in expensive designer clothes that are chosen carefully so she can deny their provenance. How does she afford these things? Her life is carefully structured—'Routine was a kind of second-order magic'—allowing her to live and work and raise her beloved son, Jun; to keep living, despite the fact she 'died' for the first time at the age of 16 when she lost her powers. Yasuko had surged into these powers aged 13:

> Then she felt a rippling nausea and slowness. It was as if everything was happening all at once but doing so at a tiny fraction of its typical speed. The first moments of her gift had a heavy quality, almost a dullness. It was the quality of inevitability.

It was then that an animal spoke to her for the first time and she understood. At 14, when she had discussed these powers with her beloved father, his face had changed, he had become frightened and ashamed. Consequently, Yasuko spent two years isolated in her room and her powers deserted her. She has been bringing up her son by herself for many years now, determinedly not engaging with any animal that looks as if it's about to say something, her daily rituals and simple life aimed at keeping the magical powers at bay.

But Yasuko knows the powers are rising again; she's both scared and excited. Her son Jun has moved out. Does she need to choose between having the powers and having him in her life? In the park a peacock speaks to her: 'We are going to help you.' Its eye is fringed and blank. 'Remain alert. We are sending you a girl.' And there is Dinah, lying on the grass in the park, fighting a migraine.

Can they, will they save each other? And what would that look like? Honest conversation, acknowledgement of hard realities, a sense of companionship on one's hard solitary journey—all might shift perspectives, ease the unbearable, allow the next step to be taken.

There were three minor things I particularly enjoyed about this book. The first is that Smaill writes so well about Japan, where I've never been, that I got curious and found myself looking up and poring over pictures of the parks and shops of Tokyo. The second is that the parts of the novel written from Yasuko's point of view *feel* Japanese, by which I mean that they read as if they have been written in Japanese and translated into English (the type of translated-from-Japanese English you might have come across in novels like *Before the Coffee Gets Cold* by Toshikazu Kawaguchi, and *She and Her Cat* by Makoto Shinkai and Naruki Nagakawa), in marked contrast to the strongly New Zealand English voice of Dinah. The third thing was when I suddenly understood why that person in the park is trying to trap a pigeon: I laughed out loud.

Smaill conjures states of deep grief and almost crippling loneliness in her characters so well, readers will be positively relieved when Yasuko and Dinah meet and connect so fast; each recognises that the other is vulnerable, damaged—barely surviving griefs and losses. Smaill has Dinah describe her grief so powerfully, I think it may be one of the best accounts I've come across: a despatch from a far country that most of us will visit eventually, if we haven't already. Dinah's life has been derailed; she seems to have landed shell-shocked in Japan without any real idea of how she got there. She likens the news of Michael's death to a train crash, where the still-living are wandering dazed in a field covered with train wreckage, while the world, a new world, keeps going:

> 'There was grass growing under the carriages. That is what surprised me the most. It was still growing. Everything was continuing on under the wreckage. Insects moving, going about their lives. Birds. Each going about their insect life, their bird life. I thought, "That's what the world is now." I knew I could never get back to the other place, where I was on a journey, going somewhere. I couldn't get back even if I tried. So … ' She shrugged. 'That's where you have to live. In that other world. The one that belongs to the grass and the birds and the insects.'
>
> Dinah thought she felt tears on her cheeks, but it was just sweat, rolling down. She didn't try to wipe it off.
>
> 'It is a very good description,' said Yasuko, 'of survival.'
>
> 'It doesn't feel like survival.'
>
> 'No.' They sat next to each other.

It is a wonderful description of the aftermath of a death, and the first time it seems that Dinah has articulated what is happening to her. Following this, her connection to Michael seems stronger, but there is also a sense that she is becoming a little tired of his dominating presence in her life. Michael is dead and she has this one life in which she has to learn to live without him. Some of her angst and distress is her guilt that before his death she was starting to do that, and she now feels she betrayed him. Yasuko, older, perhaps wiser, just laughs:

'Of course you betrayed him,' she said. 'That's how it is with people you love. It was the same with Jun and me. That doesn't make it your fault that he died.' She shook her head again.

It was remarkable that Dinah felt better. Yasuko had not known Michael or anything about their relationship, but still she felt something drift away.

Dinah's attempt to help her new friend with her own sorrow, to try to reconnect mother and son, was my least favourite part of this elegantly written novel. The son Jun is most interesting in relation to his mother; I just didn't like or care about the interactions between him and Dinah. Jun is trying to create his own life, as Dinah was before Michael died, to escape the gyre of intense familial love, obligation and exhaustion that is created when you have a person with extraordinary powers in your life.

Yasuko's powers are frightening for her, but they are also exhilarating and amazing. Michael's 'powers' are couched in terms of mental illness, while what Yasuko experiences is more ambiguously expressed. It could be a mental illness, but perhaps the animals really are talking to her? Smaill is throwing a touch of fantasy into the mix. The animals do seem to say pretty sensible, helpful things. Yasuko's apprehensive fear/delight is understandable as the author skilfully describes the first lyrical and seductive conjuring of her powers. She ends up emotionally overwhelmed 20 years later:

> Her stomach moved up into her throat. Her heart opened like a fist and started to speed. Hope waved to her like a handkerchief, far off, almost beyond her range of vision. She recognised its sharp white colour and the uptick in her bloodstream. She felt the old intoxicant drip of ego. Everything sharpened, as if she had turned a lens. No, she said. But it was impossible to stop the tide of mercy that crept up her throat and into her face.

Smaill skilfully captures the intoxicating glitter of mania—or is Yasuko finally coming into her powers? I really liked the unsettling ambiguity of the last couple of pages of the book, when we leave Dinah, who, restored to herself, is looking around at the world again, and circle back to Yasuko. There, we are confronted with the question: does Yasuko have powers or do the powers have Yasuko?

Am I Chinese Enough?
Helene Wong

Backwaters by Emma Ling Sidnam (Text Publishing, 2023), 288pp, $38

'I guess I write a lot about identity,' confesses Laura Long Stephens near the beginning of *Backwaters*. And why not? For those like her, a Chinese living in New Zealand, it's impossible not to be randomly confronted by strangers asking where you're from, and who persist when you say 'Here' with 'Yes, but where are you *really* from?' If you choose to be generous and cast this simply as well-meaning curiosity, it still signals that you're perceived as 'them' and not 'us'. Even if your family has been here for four generations.

And so Laura is—yes, let's say obsessed with—trying to get to the bottom of not only where she is really from but also who she really is, taking part in that intricate dance of escaping the one-dimensionality of her Chineseness while at the same time trying to integrate it into her unique self.

Laura is a fictional creation, the protagonist in rising New Zealand writer Emma Ling Sidnam's debut novel. The echo in their names implies autobiographical influences, and writer and character do indeed share that obsession with identity as well as both being writers, bisexual, and fourth-generation Asian New Zealanders. These are some of the filters through which *Backwaters* is told, and as a fictionalised memoir it's a refreshing addition to the growing body of literature on identity in Aotearoa.

There are as many stories about the search for identity as there are people. For most, the first port of call is whakapapa. This story, told from a fourth-generation point of view, has to navigate the distance of time and dwindling knowledge of ancestral family history. The author deals with this lack through the device of a found diary written by Laura's maternal great-great-grandfather, Kaineng (Ken), who, like other young men from southern China, sailed to New Zealand in the late nineteenth century. With her Grandpa, Ken's grandson, translating the diary for her, Laura is able to glean the outlines of her origins and, fortuitously, proceed with a writing assignment about Chinese New Zealand family histories. Although anxious about whether she's 'Chinese enough to write these stories', she's hopeful that 'writing about [race] might help me reach some conclusions about my identity'.

The diary enables Sidnam to move between Ken's past and Laura's present (set in the year before Covid), alternating vignettes of Laura's fictionalising of the diary entries with multiple subplots and throughlines from her own daily life: work, family relationships, romantic relationships, friends and fellow creatives. Narratively these are not difficult to keep track of; their brevity helps and the writing flows well. Past and present run independently of each other, however, with little provided by way of emotional or thematic connections, and along with the flatness of structure the narrative has a loose, episodic quality.

Western narratives tend to be dominated by a structure that drives the protagonist forward through conflict and the increasing tension of obstacles, then on to resolution. Non-Western and indigenous storytelling often adopts a circular structure, equally effective in drawing the reader in and on, introducing separate stories and gradually revealing their connections in a way that winds tension and suspense into the quest as well as building thematic cohesion. *Backwaters* may be attempting something of both, but the even tone and rhythm don't quite deliver that sense of rising tension.

There is one tension-generating twist, though. The revelation that one member of the family is adopted not only upends Laura's developing search for identity, it also briefly upsets the family dynamic. The depth of anger expressed, though, does not completely ring true in this age of open adoptions, whāngai customary practice and shows like *David Lomas Investigates*—especially when the family is consistently portrayed as liberal and tolerant. It feels like an overreach for the purpose of inserting conflict.

Nevertheless, there's plenty of internal conflict, which is where the wrestle with identity mainly resides. The author evokes well the confusion and ambivalence in the different arenas of Laura's life, suggesting a maze that resists and frustrates solution. She (through Laura) calls it 'bashing … against invisible walls'.

Be prepared also to experience through Laura the ambushing of one's sense of self: the eye-rolling predictability of those where-are-you-froms; the compliments on your English; the leering encounter at a bar; the aggressiveness of 'So, is it true that Asians eat dog?'

These moments are recounted with resigned amusement rather than flared nostrils. Perhaps it's because there are others in Laura's world who act as a counterweight to the stereotyping; others who 'get' her and lead her to feel she's found her tribe. It's only when circumstances take her to Hong Kong that those invisible walls start to dissolve. She finds herself part of a bigger tribe, one where she's 'us' and not 'them', and the city is where past finally meets present. As independent as Ken's story has been from Laura's, when they do touch here they bring her to an understanding and acceptance of all the facets of her true self.

Sidnam writes with clarity, frankness and a fine observation of people. In the vignettes of the past, the poet in her comes through with a more lyrical, reflective tone, and the characters seem deeper, their inner lives more thought through. Perhaps as they are inventions there was more freedom to explore. It is noticeable, though, that the characters in both stories have a tendency to sound similar, the dialogue homogenised as contemporary New Zealand rather than a variety of voices. This might be deliberate, a pointed reference to the compliments on Chinese New Zealanders' 'very good English', but distinct voices would have enhanced the reading of different characters.

There are some inauthentic elements that might have been better researched. For instance, the intimate friendship between Ken and Qiu, a young woman in his village, would very likely have been frowned upon. Villages in 1860s southern China tended to have been settled by families sharing the same surname, and such relationships between the younger generation were actively discouraged or even forbidden. A second example is when Laura gives Ken's diary to her Grandpa to translate because 'it's full of Chinese characters I can't understand'. Given the era, Ken would have written in the traditional manner with the characters to be read vertically, yet Grandpa appears to be reading them horizontally.

And there are editing stumbles—a dinner invitation for Sunday changes without explanation to Saturday; both Laura's Grandpa and his lawyer share the same name; Laura's declared vegetarianism is somewhat random. Laura's surname, Stephens, despite both her parents' Chinese origins, also goes unexplained. It's not that it's not credible, but the story behind it might have been enlightening of history or character in some useful way. These might seem minor matters, but they're jarring enough to throw an engaged reader out of a world that's been otherwise carefully drawn.

How does Laura's journey to find herself compare with those of earlier generations? Surprisingly similar, it seems. The book traverses well the stories of people, attitudes and situations that descendants of Chinese migrants (and indeed most migrants) will be familiar with when grappling with their personal mazes. And ultimately most will agree with Laura that 'These stories might be the backdrop to my life, but they don't determine who I become next.'

I Fell in Love at the Poetry Night

Iain Sharp

Rapture: An anthology of performance poetry from Aotearoa New Zealand edited by Carrie Rudzinski and Grace Iwashita-Taylor (Auckland University Press, 2023), 240pp, $59.99; **Remember Me: Poems to learn by heart from Aotearoa New Zealand** edited by Anne Kennedy (Auckland University Press, 2023), 271pp, $45

Although I've come to admire both these books and to feel grateful to their editors for enlarging my awareness of local poetry, I still grimace slightly at their titles.

Rapture? I've certainly heard performers at open mic nights who seemed besotted with their own voices, but I doubt if the editors intend their title as a euphemism for 'lost in an up-themself trance'. That would be unjust to such clear-eyed contributors as Abby Irwin-Jones (already, in her teens, a wily analyst of social interactions), Arihia Latham (beautifully poignant when expressing a young Māori mother's fears for her children's future) and Nadine Anne Hura (priceless when describing her commingled guilt and resentment as Pākehā smart-arses correct her mistakes in te reo classes).

While mood and method shift from voice to voice in the 90-strong ensemble, the tone is more often anxious or irate than ecstatic. At times, however, such as 'The Angry Poem', Penny Ashton's expletive-rich reprisal on a heckler, a gleefulness underscores the ire. Does the book's title refer to the rapture of retribution when verbal vengeance is dished out to loudmouths, racists, sexists, colonists, homophobes and other villains? Possibly, but I think Rudzinski and Iwashita-Taylor had something else in mind when they named their anthology.

The contents are split into three sections, each subtitled with an imperative redolent of self-help manuals: 'burn it down', 'float', 're-earth your roots'. In a remarkable poem towards the end of the book Daisy Speaks talks us through the application of the malu, the traditional tattoo for Samoan women. It's an agonising procedure, but the reward for those brave enough to endure it is the elation of claiming their place in the world, with their identity etched right into their skin. Among its many meanings, Speaks tells us, 'malu' can signify 'shield', 'shelter', 'protector' and 'nurturer'. I think Speaks' poem goes to the heart of what the anthology hopes to achieve. For all the sometimes-awkward humour and varying levels of technical proficiency, poetry is taken seriously here as a means of facing our demons, working through pain and discovering what we most value.

Remember Me. Who exactly is this 'me' imploring us? I think we're supposed to imagine each of the anthology's 200 poems begging to be remembered. The problem is that once I yield to this peculiar conceit I begin to hear thousands of other poems—the ones that Kennedy rejected—beseeching me from the literary graveyard. Whereas Rudzinski and Iwashita-Taylor confine themselves to the last 10 years and maintain a strict policy of one poem per poet, Kennedy roams freely across our whole printed history and observes no such quota. She has her favourites. We are offered six poems from Hone Tuwhare but nary a word from his friend and mentor R.A.K. Mason. We get five poems by James K. Baxter, but zilch by C.K. Stead, Kendrick Smithyman and Lauris Edmond. Robert Sullivan, the anthology's 'consultant te reo Māori', is accorded a tally as large as Baxter's, but we're not asked to remember anything by his contemporaries Kate Camp and James Brown. I expected Katherine Mansfield to be included since the book was published in the year of her death centennial, but she does not appear. Neither does Janet Frame. Yet Keri Hulme turns up twice.

Noting who's in and who's out is an irresistible game for us anthology reviewers, but it's a short-lived one. You pluck a book from the shelf for what it contains, after all, not what it omits. Taken on its own terms, *Remember Me* is a lot of fun, especially if you accept the challenge of committing the poems to memory. Yes, Kennedy is quirky, but she's done a fine job of mustering memorable works. Old chestnuts like 'Pōkarekare Ana', 'The Magpies' and 'Rain' are mixed with more recent gems, like Brian Turner's 'Sky', 'Charm to Get Safely Home' by Airini Beautrais and 'The Class Anxiety Country Song' by Erik Kennedy. Blasts from the past are rescued from oblivion, such as 'Ngā Rongo', Tuini Ngāwai's wonderful wartime waiata excoriating 'purari Hitara, tangata hao' ('bloody Hitler, that greedy man'). And some selections are delightfully idiosyncratic, like Nick Ascroft's 'Corpse Seeks Similar' and Murray Edmond's 'Mr Mat'.

I agree with Kennedy that nothing boosts your understanding of a poem as much as learning it by heart. I feel less sure, though, about the push towards public performance in the Afterwords by Zech Soakai and Rosalind Ali. My thespian talents don't stretch too far. I'm okay at portraying a retired librarian of Scottish extraction, since that's what I am, but I'm miscast in the roles that some of these poems demand: Samoan villager, young Irishwoman, gay Chinese poet laureate, messianic commune-leader mournfully addressing 'the small grey cloudy louse that nests in my beard'.

Inevitably, given my former profession, I tackled the anthologies in alphabetical order. There were payoffs, I found, in beginning with *Rapture*.

Rudzinski and Iwashita-Taylor lead from the front, assigning to themselves the scariest slot in any poetry reading: first up. Within a framework of controlled feminist anger, Rudzinski celebrates women's cross-generational bonds, focusing on her deep friendship with her mother despite their differing beliefs. Iwashita-Taylor draws on two key Samoan concepts: 'lagimalie' (a state of profound harmony when everything aligns) and 'va' (a simultaneous awareness that everything has its own space and everything is connected). Then, before the three-part show gets underway in earnest, the editors bring on a third introductory voice: Lyttelton writer Andy Coyle. From the title of his poem, 'I fell in love at the poetry night', I expected sugar and roses, but Coyle's perception of the poetry scene is quite unblinkered. Someone who relishes the human comedy in all its warty, flaw-filled diversity, he's ready to enjoy the 'self-obsessed hypocrites', 'exhibitionists' and 'rolling thunder type blunderers' as well as the 'shy girls', 'visionary prophets' and 'beautiful minds'. I think this is a splendid attitude to take not just to poetry nights but anywhere.

I don't know Coyle, but I want to thank him for saving me from some of my meaner impulses while perusing *Remember Me* as well as *Rapture*. I'll cite three instances.

Normally I'm a staunch fan of Ursula Bethell. Stirred, however, by the decolonising ethos of *Rapture* and on the prowl for intimations of white privilege, I found myself reacting unfavourably to her *Remember Me* poems, particularly the line in 'Compensation' about tramcar passengers arguing 'without logic'. Forgetting that Bethell died before I was born, I screamed in her general direction, 'What do you expect, you ghastly old snob!? Propositions from Wittgenstein?'

Then I recalled the Coyle Attitude and calmed down. Bethell was 55 when 'Compensation' was published—youthful compared with a septuagenarian like myself. 'Ghastly' is wrong, too, because it fails to pick up the twinkling-eyed element of self-parody in Bethell's hauteur and the deliberate hyperbole when she describes antipodean barbarity to her English pen-pal Lady Head. She called her poem 'Compensation' as a charming little tribute to her friend, for this was also the title of one of Head's novels. And even if she was mock-snobbish, Ursula wasn't too grand to use public transport.

Remember Me is a handsome book with a good font and a helpful ribbon to mark one's place, but it has some frustrating shortcomings. There's no index and no information of any kind about contributors, not even iwi affiliations for Māori authors. Surprised by the inclusion of 18th-century Ayrshire poet Robert Burns' 'To Mary in Heaven' in the anthology, presumably on the strength of Rewiti Kohere's translation 'Ki a Meri i te Rangi', I was keen to learn more, but the link provided to a Papers Past article in the book's end acknowledgments doesn't work. Grrrr!

Again, Coyle's philosophy of acceptance came to my aid. I now feel grateful to that failed URL for prompting me to dig deeper and discover Nikki Hessell's brilliant discussion of 'Ki a Meri i te Rangi' in her 2018 book

Romantic Literature and the Colonised World. Kohere was drawn to Burns, she explains, largely because of the Scot's prowess as a songwriter. Seeing connections between 'To Mary in Heaven' and traditional waiata tangi, he chose the vocabulary in his 1927 translation with care to strengthen the appeal to a Māori audience. Hessell is wise on the ways that cultural expectations shape literary taste. Rather than a single universal canon, there's a multitude of equally valid canons forged by different communities.

Which leads us to Allen Curnow and 'The Skeleton of the Great Moa in the Canterbury Museum, Christchurch'. The most canonically inclined of New Zealand's earlier anthologists, Curnow was intent on clearing away the 'trivial if sincere' dross, as he saw it, and promoting the work he considered most important—his own and that of his friends and associates. All 19 contributors to his *Book of New Zealand Verse 1923–45* were Pākehā, all were from British stock, and 17 were male.

Having hitherto accepted Curnow at his own high valuation, I was surprised when memorising 'The Skeleton of the Moa' by how clumsy an attempt at a Shakespearean sonnet it is, with its unmetrical 13-syllable opening line, its succession of horrible off-rhymes (crutches/hatches, swamp/damp, islands/Zealand's, and so on) and its concluding couplet where you have to elide the middle part of the adjective 'marvellous' and say 'MAHV'luz', like some posh twit in a P.G. Wodehouse story, or else the iambic rhythm comes unsprung. Rather than this realisation lowering Curnow in my esteem, however, I've begun to warm to him now that I no longer regard him as an irreproachable master prosodist but place him in the more lovable category of Kiwi do-it-yourselfers whose constructions are not quite as flash as they think.

So fixated is Curnow on white settler experience that it never crosses his mind in this sonnet to ask whether any Māori succeeded in 'standing upright here'. His erasure of tangata whenua from the picture is so complete that it becomes comical, especially when he attributes the demise of the moa not to over-enthusiastic hunting but to an evolutionary flaw ('interesting failure to adapt on islands').

There's no point remonstrating with Curnow. He's gone, and so is his conception of New Zealand. You have only to glance at all the female, Māori, Pasifika, Islamic, Asian, American and LGBTQIA+ contributors included in both these anthologies to see how much the publishing world has changed since Curnow's heyday. We can afford to smile at his spectre and love him, Andy Coyle-style, as a product (a MAHV'luz product, let's concede) of his culture and time, as we all are.

INTRODUCING OUR ONLINE SALE!

A selection of beautiful books at heavily discounted prices

www.scorpiobooks.co.nz

NEW AND UPCOMING FROM OTAGO UNIVERSITY PRESS

OUT NOW

Heart Stood Still
by Miriam Sharland

Bob Crowder: A New Zealand Organics Pioneer
by Matt Morris

COMING SOON

Echoes from Hawaiki: The origins and development of Māori and Moriori musical instruments
by Jennifer Cattermole

Power to Win: The Living Wage Movement in Aotearoa New Zealand
by Lyndy McIntyre

Find out more at oup.nz

Proudly supporting poetry since the '80s.

We've been putting poetry on posters for decades.

From the heart of New Zealand to American streets and famous spots around Europe, sharing poetry is part of the Phantom Billstickers legacy.

CASELBERG TRUST INTERNATIONAL poetry PRIZE 2024

Supported by **UNIVERSITY BOOK SHOP**

FIRST PRIZE: $500
+ one week stay at the Caselberg House, Broad Bay, Dunedin

SECOND PRIZE: $250

HIGHLY COMMENDED
(no monetary prize)

2024 judge: **ALAN RODDICK**
ENTRIES OPEN: **1 June 2024**
ENTRIES CLOSE: **31 July 2024**

The first and second placed poems will be published in the November 2024 edition of Landfall

For Conditions & Entry Form:
www.caselbergtrust.org

The Landfall Essay Competition 2024

THE LANDFALL ESSAY COMPETITION seeks to encourage Aotearoa writers to continue the tradition of vivid, contentious and creative essay writing.

ENTRIES will be judged by *Landfall* editor Lynley Edmeades and the winner will receive $3000 and a year's subscription to *Landfall*. The winning essay will be published in *Landfall 248*. Entries also have the chance of publication in *Strong Words: The best of the Landfall Essay Competition*.

PAST WINNERS INCLUDE Siobhan Harvey, Tina Makereti, Andrew Dean, A.M. McKinnon, Tobias Buck, Nina Mingya Powles, Alice Miller, Laurence Fearnley, Alie Benge, Airini Beautrais and Tracey Slaughter.

SUBMISSIONS CLOSE 31 JULY

For more information go to:
oup.nz/landfall-essay-comp

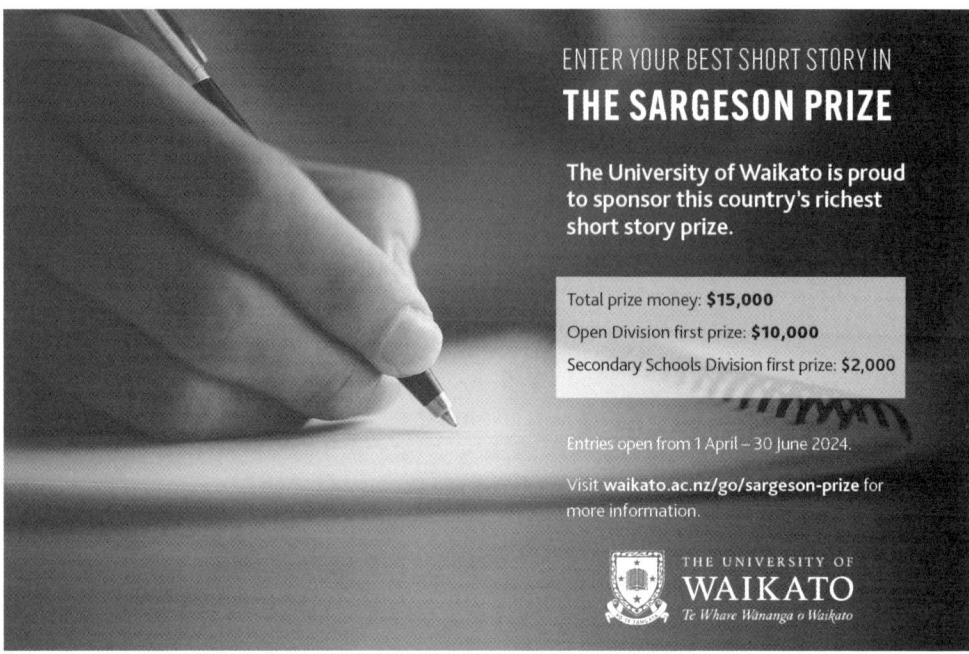

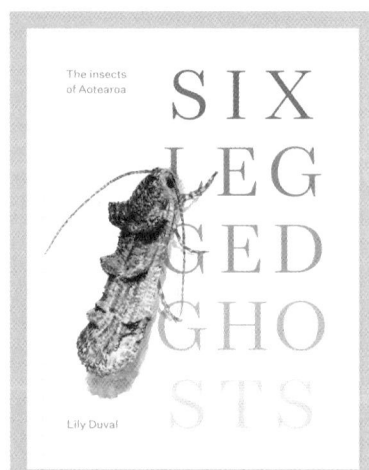

Six-legged Ghosts: The insects of Aotearoa
Lily Duval

$55, HB, 296pp, full colour

Richly illustrated and including more than 100 original paintings by the author, *Six-legged Ghosts* examines the art, language, stories and science of insects in Aotearoa and around the world.

Moving between te ao Māori and the medieval art world, between museum displays and stories of the insect apocalypse, extinction and conservation, Lily Duval explores the lives of insects not only in the natural environments of Aotearoa but in our cultures and histories as well.

Available from all good bookshops   Published with the support of Creative New Zealand

www.canterbury.ac.nz/cup

SOME THINGS WRONG
Thomas Pors Koed

"There aren't enough experimental Édouard Levé-esque books published in Aotearoa. Koed creates a claustrophobic narrative with a rhythm built on staccato sentences, guilt, and repetition. ... Koed describes himself as writing 'unpopular fiction' but all I say is: More please!"
— Brannavan Gnanalingam

The Spinoff: 'The Aotearoa books of the year for 2023'

VOLUME EDITIONS
VOLUME.NZ/editions   books@volume.nz

UNIVERSITY BOOK SHOP
For all booklovers, *everywhere.*

Visit us soon in our newly refurbished store

378 Great King Street, Dunedin | Open 7 Days
Ph 03 477 6976 | unibooks.co.nz

CONTRIBUTORS

Nicola Andrews (Ngāti Paoa, Pākehā) is a Māori writer currently living on Ramaytush Ohlone territory. They are the winner of the 2023 AAALS Indigenous Writers Prize for Poetry. Their debut chapbook, Māori Maid Difficult, is out now with Tram Editions.

Nick Ascroft's most recent collection, The Stupefying (Te Herenga Waka University Press), was named best poetry book of 2022 by Newsroom. It will not be his last. Apologies.

Rebecca Ball is a poetry and prose writer from just outside Ōtautahi. She has had work published in journals and anthologies, including Landfall, London Grip, Turbine | Kapohau and Poetry Aotearoa Yearbook.

Maddie Ballard is a writer from Tāmaki Makaurau. Her work has been published in titles including Turbine | Kapohau and Starling. Her debut essay collection, Bound: A Memoir of Making and Remaking, will be published by The Emma Press in 2024.

Airini Beautrais lives in Whanganui. She is the author of an award-winning collection of short stories, Bug Week, four collections of poetry, and the essay collection The Beautiful Afternoon (THWUP 2024).

Lucinda Birch is a writer and artist whose work has been published in various anthologies, including Sport and Landfall. The four pieces in this issue, 'Seeing Things,' are part of a larger collection of stories and photographs due to be published in 2025.

Cindy Botha lives in Tauranga. Her poems appear in magazines and anthologies in the UK, USA, Australia and NZ.

Amy Brown is from Aotearoa and now lives in Australia. She has published three collections of poetry and four children's novels. Her debut novel for adults, My Brilliant Sister, was released by Scribner in January 2024.

Connie Buchanan is a Hamilton writer and deputy editor of E-Tangata magazine. Her work has also appeared in Newsroom, Headland, The Spinoff and NZ Geographic. She is studying creative writing at Waikato University.

Nathaniel Calhoun works at the intersection of biodiversity and artificial intelligence from his home in Aotearoa New Zealand.

Chris Cantillon lives in Whanganui and works in Marton and has been reading and writing poetry since he was nineteen.

Lorraine Carmody lives in rural Canterbury with her horses, dogs, sheep and cattle. She is halfway through an MA in creative writing.

CONTRIBUTORS

Medb Charleton is originally from Ireland. Her poetry has been published previously in *Landfall*, *Sport*, *Poetry New Zealand* and online. She is currently undertaking a PhD in English at the University of Waikato.

Thom Conroy is the author of the novels *The Salted Air* (Penguin Random House, 2016) and *The Naturalist* (2014) and the editor of the essay collection *Home* (Massey University Press, 2017). His short fiction has been recognised by Best American Short Stories and received other awards, including the Katherine Ann Porter Prize in Fiction. He is a senior lecturer in creative writing at Massey University and the editor-in-chief of the journal *Headland*.

Brett Cross lives in the Waikato where he runs two small publishing presses. He has previously published work in several journals, including *Cordite*, *Poetry New Zealand* and *Brief*.

Michelle Duff is a journalist and fiction writer from Feilding who lives in Pōneke. In 2023, she won the International Institute of Modern Letters Fiction Prize.

Mark Edgecombe is a church pastor in Tawa. His poems have appeared in journals in Australia and New Zealand.

David Eggleton is a poet and writer based in Ōtepoti Dunedin. His most recent book is *Respirator: Laureate Poems 2019–2022*, published by Otago University Press.

Michelle Elvy is a writer, editor and teacher of creative writing in Ōtepoti Dunedin. Her most recent work includes *A Kind of Shelter: Whakaruru-taha*, an anthology edited with Witi Ihimaera (Massey University Press, 2023).

Joan Fleming's latest book is the verse novel *Song of Less* (Cordite Books, 2022), which imagines the limits of love, language and individualism in the ruins of ecological collapse.

Craig Foltz is a writer and photographer whose work has appeared in numerous journals and anthologies (*Conjunctions*, *Diagram* and *Fence*, among others). He is the author of three books of poetry and prose, the most recent of which is the collection *Locals Only* (Compound Press, 2020). He currently lives and works in New Plymouth.

Ayesha Green (Kāi Tahu, Ngāti Kahungunu) is an artist based in Aotearoa. Her practice explores mātauraka Māori, nation building and the relationship between the empire and indigeneity.

Michael Hall lives in Dunedin. He grew up on the Rangitāiki Plains.

David Herkt is an Auckland-based writer and former TV producer. His literary and journalistic work has been widely published. He has been a winner of the

Sunday Star-Times Short Story Competition and his TV productions have gained two Media and Television Awards: Best Documentary Series and Best Children's Programme.

Chris Holdaway is a poet, publisher and translator. He is the author of *Gorse Poems* (Titus Books, 2022), and his translation from the French of Léon-Paul Fargue's *Vulturne* is forthcoming from Contra Mundum Press. He directs the award-winning poetry publishing outfit Compound Press.

Emma Hughes was raised in Auckland and studied Commerce and Arts at Victoria University of Wellington. Emma works as an HR Advisor and is passionate about music and storytelling. She mainly writes YA fiction and poetry and is moving to London to see the world.

Mia-Francesca Jones is a writer, PhD candidate and recipient of the William Thomas Williams Postgraduate Scholarship. Her work explores homesickness, climate change, motherhood and meteorology.

Greg Judkins is a retired doctor and medical educator. He has used creative writing to promote empathy in young doctors and has published collections of poems and short fiction.

Kristin Kelly is a Wellington bureaucrat who struggles to repurpose her creative writing into policy advice. She lives in Newtown with her large, poorly-behaved dog.

Fiona Kidman has published six collections of poetry over the past 50 or so years. She also writes novels, memoirs and essays. Her home is in Mount Victoria, Wellington, overlooking the sea.

Pat Kraus is a self-taught photographer and musician from Tāmaki Makaurau. His 2023 exhibition of 'failed portraiture' *(Ghost/Portraits)*, was the inaugural show at the newly-opened gallery, Stepdown, in Heretaunga Hastings.

Wes Lee lives in Wellington and has three poetry collections. In 2022, she was awarded the Heroines/Joyce Parkes Women's Writing Prize in New South Wales. In 2023, she was shortlisted for the Kathleen Grattan Poetry Award and The Poetry London Pamphlet Prize.

Zoë Meager's work has appeared in *Cheap Pop, Ellipsis Zine, Granta, Hue and Cry, Landfall, Lost Balloon, Mascara Literary Review, Mayhem, Meniscus, North & South, Overland, Splonk* and *Turbine | Kapohau*, among others. She is a 2024 Sargeson Fellow.

Scott Menzies is Pākehā of Scottish, English and Irish decent. His fiction has appeared in *Landfall, takahē* and *The Commuting Book* among other places. His story 'One Hundred' was shortlisted for the inaugural Secret Lives competition.

CONTRIBUTORS

Harvey Molloy lives in Wellington. He is the author of three books of poetry: *Night Music* (2018), *Udon by The Remarkables* (2016) and *Moonshot* (2008). He is also the co-author, with Latika Vasil, of the book *Asperger Syndrome, Adolescence, and Identity: Looking beyond the label*.

Federico Monsalve is an Auckland-based journalist and editor. His work has appeared in most major New Zealand print media outlets and a smattering of international ones.

Emma Neale is an Ōtepoti Dunedin-based writer and freelance editor. She is the author of thirteen books of fiction and poetry.

Mikaela Nyman writes poetry, fiction and non-fiction. Co-editor of *Sista, Stanap Strong! A Vanuatu Women's Anthology* (Te Herenga Waka University Press, 2021). Her second poetry collection in Swedish is nominated for the Finnish Broadcasting Company YLE's Literature Prize 2023. She's the 2024 Robert Burns Fellow.

Simone Oettli is an independent scholar currently living in Geneva, Switzerland.

Claire Orchard (she/her) lives in Te Whanganui-a-Tara and is the author of two poetry collections, *Cold Water Cure* (Victoria University Press, 2016) and *Liveability* (Te Herenga Waka University Press, 2023).

James O'Sullivan is a writer living in New Plymouth, who writes plays, short stories and novels.

James Pasley is a writer from Auckland. His writing has appeared in *Landfall, Newsroom, Sunday Star-Times, Metro* and *Los Angeles Review of Books*, among others.

Vaughan Rapatahana (Te Ātiawa) commutes between homes in Hong Kong, the Philippines, and Aotearoa New Zealand. He is widely published across several genres in both his main languages, te reo Māori and English, and his work has been translated into Bahasa Malaysian, Italian, French, Mandarin, Romanian and Spanish. He is the author and editor of well over forty books.

Harry Ricketts has published around thirty books, most recently *Selected Poems* (Te Herenga Waka Press, 2021). He teaches a creative non-fiction course at the International Institute of Modern Letters and lives in Wellington.

Iain Sharp was a frequent participant at Auckland's Poetry Live events in the 1980s and '90s. He has published five books of poetry and his work has appeared in several anthologies.

Nicola Thorstensen is an Ōtepoti poet. She is a member of the Octagon Poetry Collective, which organises monthly poetry readings. She recently completed a Master of Creative Writing through Massey University. Her work explores personal experience through a political lens.

Ariana Tikao (Kāi Tahu) is a musician and writer living in Ōtautahi. She is a 2023 Ursula Bethell Writer in Residence at the University of Canterbury and an Arts Laureate.

Chris Tse is the New Zealand Poet Laureate for 2022–25. His most recent collection is *Super Model Minority* (Auckland University Press, 2022).

Kate van der Drift is a contemporary photographer working and living between Tāmaki Makaurau Auckland and Whāingaroa Raglan. She has a particular interest in recording and highlighting the ecological and environmental effects of human intervention on land and waterscapes.

Lauren Vargo is a Research Fellow and Marsden Grant recipient at the Antarctic Research Centre, Wellington. Her research explores how and why ice and snow (particularly glaciers) are changing.

Ian Wedde's memoir, *The Grass Catcher: A Digression About Home*, was published in 2014, his *Selected Poems* in 2017, and his novel *The Reed Warbler* in 2020. He won the Landfall Essay Prize in 2010. *The Social Space of the Essay 2003–2023*, a new collection of his non-fiction writing, is forthcoming from Te Herenga Waka University Press.

Rose Whitau is Kāi Tahu, Waitaha, Kāti Mamoe and Pākehā. She lives in Wadandi Boodja in Western Australia with her partner, their two kids and their dog. Her poems have appeared in *Landfall*, *Turbine | Kapohau* and *takahē*.

Jessica Wilkinson is a creative writing academic at RMIT University and the author of three poetic biographies—*Marionette: A biography of Miss Marion Davies*, *Suite for Percy Grainger* and *Music Made Visible: A biography of George Balanchine*.

Kit Willett is an Auckland-based English teacher, poet and executive editor of the Aotearoa poetry journal *Tarot*. His debut poetry collection, *Dying of the Light*, was published by Resource Publications in 2022.

Helene Wong has worked in film, television and theatre as an actor, writer, director, script consultant and critic. She is a third-generation Chinese New Zealander with a keen interest in the stories of Asian migrants, and in 2016 her memoir *Being Chinese: a New Zealander's Story* was published by Bridget Williams Books.

Kirby Wright was born and raised in Hawaii, where he spent summers with his hapa haole grandmother on her Moloka'i horse ranch. He has been a guest lecturer at Trinity College, Dublin.

Nicholas Wright teaches literature and creative writing at Te Whare Wānanga o Waitaha, Ōtautahi. His poetry has been published in *Landfall*, *takahē*, *Otoliths*, *The Spinoff* and *Poetry Aotearoa Yearbook*. He is currently writing a book of essays on poetry in Aotearoa.

Phoebe Wright is a writer of poems, stories and occasionally non-fiction, originally from Ōtautahi and now living in Whakaraupō Lyttelton. She has published work in *Landfall*, *takahē*, the National Library Blog, *Stuff*, *The Six Pack*, *Bonsai*, *Turbine | Kapohau*, *Starling* and *The Butterfly Diaries*.

Bronwyn Wylie-Gibb has been a bookseller and book buyer in independent bookshops in Aotearoa and the UK for thirty-six years, most recently at the Otago University Bookshop. She has also served as a Fiction Prize judges' convenor at the Ockham New Zealand Book Awards.

Zephyr Zhang 张挚 is a writer and performer based in Tāmaki Makaurau. They have poems published in various literary caves and crevasses including *Starling*, *Sweet Mammalian* and *The Spinoff*.

CONTRIBUTIONS

Landfall publishes original poems, essays, short stories, excerpts from works of fiction and non-fiction in progress, reviews, articles on the arts, and portfolios by artists. Submissions must be emailed to landfall@otago.ac.nz with 'Landfall submission' in the subject line.

For further information visit our website oup.nz/landfall

SUBSCRIPTIONS

Landfall is published in May and November. The subscription rates for 2024 (two issues) are: New Zealand $55 (including GST); Australia $NZ65; rest of the world $NZ70. Sustaining subscriptions help to support New Zealand's longest running journal of arts and letters, and the writers and artists it showcases. These are in two categories: Friend: between $NZ75 and $NZ125 per year. Patron: $NZ250 and above.

Send subscriptions to Otago University Press, PO Box 56, Dunedin, New Zealand. For enquiries, email landfall@otago.ac.nz or call 64 3 479 8807.

Print ISBN: 978-1-99-004877-7
ePDF ISBN: 978-1-99-004878-4
ISSN 00–23–7930

Copyright © Otago University Press 2024

Published by Otago University Press
533 Castle Street, Dunedin
New Zealand

Typeset by Otago University Press.
Printed in New Zealand by Caxton.

Pat Kraus, *Modesty (Portrait of Zarah Butcher-McGunnigle)*, 2022. Image courtesy of the artist.